The Final Months of Hoo-hah

A N

Koren Cowgill

Acknowledgements:

I offer heartfelt thanks to those who supported and helped me with the process of writing *The Final Months of Hoo-hah*, especially Ron and members of his writing workshop, Chris, Jane, Jim, Scott and Steve. I also thank my Mom, sisters Kathy and Kali, and cousin Michael for reading through rough drafts, and thanks to my sister, Kali Cowgill, who created the beautiful cover art. Finally, I thank my dear husband Richard, for his enduring sense of humor and kindness.

Cover Artwork:

Kali Cowgill

Dedicated with Love to Richard

Koren Cowgill is a composer, mezzo-soprano and writer, who holds undergraduate and doctoral degrees from the Eastman School of Music and a masters degree from Yale, all degrees in music composition. As a mezzo-soprano, she performs as a soloist in venues throughout Southern NJ, appearing in Menotti's operas *The Medium* and *Amahl and the Night Visitors*. In addition, Miss Cowgill sings with the Doug Murdock Meistersingers. As a composer, she participated in the Norfolk, CT Chamber Music and Aspen Music festivals. Her works for orchestra and chamber ensembles have been premiered in and out of the academic community. Miss Cowgill has been a lecturer in the Cape May County library system, where she presented "Operatic Adventures I and II." Her lecture, "Music in Film," was sponsored by the Avalon Free Public Library. As music director of the Seven Mile Island Singers, she provides entertainment for community events and nursing homes. Koren completed her novel, *The Final Months of Hoo-hah*, in 2019. Her short *Christmas Ghost Stories I and II* can be found on Amazon. Koren lives in Cape May County with her husband, Richard, and their dog, Saffron.

Koren Cowgill

The Final Months of Hoo-hah

Chapter One
Saturday, October 17, 2015
3:51 pm

Thwack!

The ball sails over the fairway and approaches the flag, slicing to the right of the green and into the water. You grimace, stomp your foot and move aside. "Damn pond." You turn to Coach. "I need some time—to think about it."

He shakes his head and practices his swing. You love the slow backswing and the whoosh of his follow-through. Khaki shorts fit snug on his bottom; an orange golf shirt stretches across broad shoulders.

"I'm about to turn seventy-one, Alex." He points at the red markers. "You should use the women's tees."

Sexy—even when irritated.

"If I ever play golf with a woman, I'll tee off from there. And you're not old," you say.

Coach drives the ball and it lands on the green near the flag. "Time is running out."

"You—we—have plenty of time. Your family—"

"What they think doesn't matter. We love each other. If you don't want a big wedding, we can elope," he says.

"I'm not ready," you say.

"You're being selfish."

"I'm sorry," you mutter.

"Let's get moving." He picks up the bag and walks down the fairway.

The car is quiet. You look out the window, wiping tears away with the sleeve of your shirt. Coach pulls into a space in your condominium complex and rests his hand on your knee. You turn to him and place your hand on his, squeeze it and get out of the car.

Before you open the condo door, you peek in the window. *Aha.* You put the key in, quiet and stealthy, and open the door. "Jefferson." He lifts his head but doesn't bother to stir from his position on the couch. "Jeffrey." You crack a smile. He yawns and rolls on his back, stretches and jumps down. "C'mon."

You gave him a bath the other day and his black, tan and white beagle coloring almost sparkles—his whites are whiter and his browns are brighter. You smile for real and open the slider to let him out. A squirrel runs for the evergreen trees and bushes to avoid him, and he forages in the grass until he takes care of business.

You let him in and pour his chow into a bowl. As you open the refrigerator Jefferson sits beside you, waiting. He'll have what you're having. "Sorry to disappoint you, Sweet-pea." You close the fridge, foregoing dinner.

A shower doesn't help and you're sweaty as you dress. Your gut aches where Coach's comment about selfishness stabbed you. The hoo-hah is under the kitchen sink, where you hide it from yourself as well as everyone else. You pour two shots into a coffee cup. Nothing makes you feel better except feeling nothing at all.

5:03 pm

You didn't drink enough and you're restless. The evening is mild so you grab your purse and go for a walk. After a mile, you approach the church. You can make part of Saturday evening mass.

The church sprawls, an English Tudor-type building. Once inside you glance at the ceiling, which is high and looks like the hull of a ship. You sit in the back row to avoid people, afraid they'll smell the whiskey on your breath.

Mass isn't sung Saturday evenings. You'll have to go again in the morning when you sing with the choir for the music service. Church is grueling. The people are nice enough, but the rigmarole gets to you. The choir sings with the organ from the loft at the back of the church, or with the piano in front, between the altar and the congregation. You all have to run up and down the stairs throughout the service. You're always out of breath. The choir robes, scratchy and cumbersome, weigh on you. Maybe Father will spring for new robes.

This evening you hope to get more out of the service without the hustle and bustle of choir activities. Sunday mornings you're there because the church pays you to lead the alto section. You always sit alone in the back row of the loft behind the church choir ladies and do your job.

"The Lord be with you."

"And also with you," the congregation says.

When it's time for communion you walk to the front of the church, where you kneel before the altar, and wait your turn. Father moves along the rail doling out the host, eventually coming to you. The wafer feels like cardboard in your mouth. The acolyte places the cup to your lips; you drink then chew, allowing the liquid to wash the stale taste away. The wine usually gives you a little shiver in the morning; now it turns your stomach. Tears form in your eyes.

In your seat once again, you remember how you first met Coach two years ago here in church when you sang for a wedding. As you stood in line to greet the bride and groom after the service, the church's secretary introduced you.

"Max, this is Alex, our songbird," she said, hands aflutter, and then she flitted away.

You blushed.

"Your voice is powerful," Max said.

"Yes, I'm loud."

"I meant you sound beautiful."

"Sometimes it's difficult to sing for these things. Weddings, funerals, christenings, I cry at all of them—doesn't matter."

"You held up okay today."

"They paid me heaps of cash." You smiled and he laughed. "How do you know the family?" you said.

"I work with the bride's mother. We both teach English."

"I often wish I did something useful."

Then a man interrupted your conversation. "Hey, Coach. Great game yesterday."

"Thanks. We finally have a winning season. Do you know Alex?" Max said, turning to you.

"Haven't had the pleasure. Nice singing," the man said.

You forced yourself to be gracious. "Thank you."

They continued to talk and you stood aside, wondering what to do with yourself.

Coach.

You liked his face. His hearty laugh reminded you of your Nana's, an infectious laugh that makes the entire face light up. In spite of yourself, you smiled, watching him talk. He caught you smiling, excused himself and started towards you, then panic welled up in your stomach.

"Are you going to the reception?"

"I wasn't going to," you said.

"You have other plans."

"N-no."

"So, I'll see you there?" he said.

You didn't know how to respond. He wasn't arrogant, but his easy confidence tugged at you. Before you could stop yourself, you said, "That'll be nice, thanks."

You ended up at the same table and danced with him all evening. That was two years ago.

Now, sitting in church you fret because he wants to marry you—such a hardship. Any normal woman would feel blessed to marry a good guy like that. But not you. You're the anomaly, the ingrate, the weirdo.

6:46 pm

After mass, you leave before anyone tries to talk to you. The brisk walk gives you energy, but you need to dampen your senses again. When you come to the restaurant with the package store in the back where you usually get your booze, you go in.

The stool grates on the floor as you drag it back. You sit and look over your shoulder. Nobody notices.

"What'll it be?" the bartender says.

"Long Island iced-tea, thanks."

"Comin' right up."

You stand and take off your coat, careful not to disturb the barstool again in spite of country music blaring over the din of conversation.

The bartender returns, bringing your drink. "I've seen you in the store, but not the bar."

"Yeah, I usually don't drink in bars." The whiskey you already drank loosened your tongue and you wince.

"Let me know if you need anything." He busies himself with other customers.

You drink the gussied-up "tea" and order another.

The bartender squints at you. "Are you driving?"

"No, I walked."

You take more time with the second, sipping as you listen to the man on your right talking on his cell phone. His deep voice has an accent. "I will do it. Yes. I will do it in the night, this night, or the next." He slouches toward the bar and thumps his elbow on it. With his head resting on in his hand, he gives you a grin.

You look away, and turn back; his eyes linger on your butt, his pointy brows raised.

"*Bon soir*," he says.

"Good evening," you return. "But you're not French."

"*Nem*," he says. "Hungarian. But I have the French language."

"Hungarian. And you speak English and French."

"It is a common thing." He sings along with the song playing on the sound system, his voice an octave lower than the country crooner's voice.

You smile. His accent makes the words to the song even more comical.

"You like this music?" he says.

"Quite honestly, no."

"Why not? It is sincere and expresses sorrow."

"It's whiny. Wah, wah, wah. I hate the twang and repetition, and how the words rhyme."

"You do not like poetry?"

"This is hardly poetry."

The man's phone rings. He pushes a stray strand of hair over his ear, gets up and saunters toward the door, and you have the opportunity to check him out. The restaurant is dark. It's hard to tell how tall he is. His hair, pulled back, hangs below the collar of his leather jacket.

Ponytailed men—gross.

The bartender returns and watches the man leave. "That guy again," he says, shaking his head.

"You know him?"

"Yes. He's been coming here a lot lately—drinks a clear soda with a cherry every time—"

"What's wrong with that?" you say.

"He sits at the bar but never drinks any alcohol. Mostly, he talks on the phone, although if a customer gets too close he'll spout off in some other language and they'll leave real fast."

"Thanks."

"Can I get you anything else?"

"I'll have a shot of Jack in a coffee this time."

"Certainly," he says.

The man returns, walking slowly toward you. "I must leave soon. Please. What is your name?"

You're flattered but hesitate. "Fifi."

He laughs. "You will not tell me. It is all right. I like that you are not skinny and straight, like a post. Your blue eyes and hair—Black Irish, no? I am Zoltán."

"Thanks to the good old Spanish Armada." You pull your skirt over your knees.

"You will walk with me, yes?"

You meet his brown eyes, so light they're almost gold.

9:25 pm

"*Mon Dieu!*" Zoltán moans, his deep voice sending a delicious jolt through your body.

Hiked up around your waist, the skirt bunches up at your belly. You straddle him as his hands clutch at your shoulders. He thrusts up into you, head thrown back against the seat. You groan, trying as hard as you can, but the alcohol makes you dull and you can't find the right groove to make it happen. And the condom doesn't help.

Sweat pours out of your skin; guilt seethes in your stomach.

Coach.

Your soaked blouse sticks to you and Zoltán tugs at it. You pull the blouse over your head and throw it behind the seat.

People approach the car next door, and you remember Zoltán's SUV has tinted windows. They get in their car and pull away, and you wonder if they noticed the shaking vehicle.

"You feel good?" Zoltán says, continuing to pump under you.

You want it to feel good, but you're numb. Not much of a faker, you either do with cataclysmic glee or don't at all.

"I'm sorry."

"Too much drink. Try something new. How about the white line? You like coke? You take that and we go again, yes?" he says.

Ick!

"No, thanks." You fumble at your skirt, smoothing it down. "I have to go."

"Very well. I see you again?"

"Sure," you lie, and reach across the seat, feeling around for your blouse.

"I am sad you leave so soon."

"Sorry."

He smiles—intriguing, but with lupine toothiness in the midst of a full beard and mustache.

You shiver, struggling to get your top on. "See you around."

"Yes. I see you again," he says.

You skulk out of the SUV and glance around the parking lot. *Whew.* The walk home clears your senses but once you're there, tired and cold, your mind is still cranked up. You hurry to the kitchen sink, open the cabinet and look behind cleaning products and plastic bags you've failed to recycle. Your body shakes and you take a drink of Jack Daniels.

Must. Tell. Someone.

Your first impulse is to call Coach and spill your guts. But that would be selfish, tattling on yourself to make you feel better at his expense. You get a second glass, this one bigger, and fill it with whiskey. Both tumbler and glass sit next to your computer and you pray your father's available. With FaceTime open, you select Professor Mac and hit the call button.

"Ally! Good to see you." your father says, loosening his tie.

"Hi, Dad."

"What brings you at this late hour? And a day early, too." He reaches out with a glass in his hand and you stretch your glass to his. "Clink," he says. "What are we drinking tonight?"

"You know what I drink, Dad."

"I really must send you something better. This Glen Garioch is quite lovely," he says and puts the glass near his nose, inhaling deeply. "I swear the fumes are enough to do the trick."

"Well, I need a bit more than the aroma."

"Now, what's wrong, Dear?"

"Da-ad," you say and start to cry.

You tell him everything, from your refusal to marry Coach, to church and the stale host, to meeting Zoltán.

Quiet for a while, your father sighs and scratches his head. "Cocaine, eh? Ally, you must never, ever tell Max."

"But I have to tell someone else. You're too easy on me."

"There's no need. I forgive you, and God does, too," he says.

"You don't count and God doesn't care."

"You're a child of God as much as anyone. He does care. Try to see the situation as an opportunity for spiritual growth."

"I blew this opportunity," you say.

"It's what you learn that will help you grow. And sometimes we need to find out what we don't want."

"Oh, Dad."

"Go to sleep, Child. You need rest."

Thursday, October 22
4:27 pm

The aluminum bench flexes as you plop on it and people down the row from you stare. You hunch into the wind, trying to make yourself smaller. Crowds line the home team bleachers. The game is almost over, but you can say you were there.

The day is cold for late October. You tug at the collar of your blouse, letting cool air in, and peer into your cleavage.

A voice you recognize shouts at Coach. "Play number forty-seven! He has not had a chance!"

Zoltán! Where's his creepy facial hair?

Coach doesn't hear him and continues speaking to the huddle. The boys disperse for the next play and Coach steps off the field.

"Come. On. Put László in," Zoltán grumbles and sits, muttering to himself.

You shudder and hope he won't see you.

László remains on the side as the defense pushes the offensive line into the backfield. The home crowd cheers and the clock runs down to zero. You stay seated as happy crowds file off the bleachers. Zoltán turns and gathers his things. His eyes connect with yours; he looks you over and you face the other way. When you stand to leave he's gone.

6:32 pm

Over dinner you listen, or try to, in the midst of your shame. Coach's face becomes animated while he talks and the lines around his green eyes are attractive, a life of smiling. "I try to get to know the parents, too. The kids are easy. These days the parents hover more, and you have to watch how you discipline the kids. They're good people though."

The waitress arrives. You cringe and lower your head, but glance at her on the sly as you pretend to peruse the menu. She's tall and reserved, dressed in black, elegant and lithe. Coach smiles at her and orders first. He'll have the grilled salmon over salad. They look to you. Your cotton top feels like wet plaster.

"Are you ready to order?" the waitress says.

You try to smile. The corners of your mouth will not cooperate, and they tremble.

"What'll you have, Honey?" Coach says.

"Same thing, thanks." You excuse yourself and head to the ladies' room.

You finish, dab your face with a towel, and wash your hands. The mirror is cruel; it shows a red face with blue eyes, a sweat-speckled complexion in a cloud of black hair with white roots showing. Most of your lipstick has rubbed off. Tears well up and you blink them away, reposition your scarf so it hides the blotchy skin between your open collars, and leave the restroom.

As you approach the table, you see Coach laughing with the waitress. Her back is toward you; you can tell she's amused. You'd like to hate him for being so nice, so attentive to the waitress, but he's that way with everyone.

You pause near the table and hope she'll go away before you sit. Aware of the extra pounds you carry, you yank your shirttail over your butt.

Coach looks around the young woman, sees you, and smiles. Because his smile is contagious, you return it. He focuses on you as you sit and the waitress leaves.

"Hey, our waitress graduated a couple years back. I don't remember her but she played varsity lacrosse."

"Wherever we go, you always make a new friend, or see someone you know."

"Isn't that a good thing?" he says, and laughs.

You roll your eyes.

The food arrives. After a few tentative bites, you eat in earnest. Coach watches you. "I'm glad you're eating. You need to, especially when you're working so hard."

"I don't work that hard. It's not even work, and I do it at home."

"Just because you like what you do doesn't mean it's not work."

"Okay," you say.

"Want me to come by tonight?"

You want to say yes. You want that smile aimed at you again. But fear erupts in your stomach. You think of Zoltán, then the soaked bedclothes, and how you must fling the covers back to let the fan cool you off. You feel tainted—your body, your skin, your mind, your heart.

You'll never drink again.

"Uh, no, thanks." You attempt to brighten your face and emit an aura of bubbly and fun, so you bounce in your seat. "How about tomorrow night after the game? Friday night is better."

And you'll find a priest and confess.

Coach buys it. "I'll look forward to it."

Relief washes over you when his kind eyes light up.

9:13 pm

The clock on the dresser gives off a red glow that creeps you out in the dark. You reach across the bed and turn on the light, wishing you had told Coach to come over. Your tablet sits on a shelf across the room, a gift from Coach. The book on your nightstand isn't interesting and you consider using the tablet. Stubborn, and still stuck in the idea that books are precious—the feel of them, the fact that you can spill coffee on them and not worry, make notes in them and feel how far you've read and have left—you pick up the paperback. The phone startles you.

"Hello?"

"Hi," Coach says.

"Hey."

"I was worried about you."

"I'm sorry. I wasn't with it today. But I'm better now," you say.

"You'll be alright, then," he says.

"Sure wish I had said yes."

"What?"

"Wish I said yes."

"That's what I thought you said. Just had my shower so I'll be right there. Oh, and—"

"What?"

"Should I take a blue pill?"

You can change your mind again and slosh yourself with booze instead.

"Alex?" he says.

But you said you weren't going to do that anymore.

"Sure. See you soon," you say.

"Great."

You jump out of bed and race to the bathroom. A wave of heat lingers on your pajamas, and you peel them off. The shower is too hot, and you turn the knob to cool the stream. You soap your body and hope you don't sweat any more, at least until he arrives. You rinse your hair, realizing you're taking too long when the doorbell rings. Coach has a key, so you finish and towel off. You leave your hair damp and dress, finding Coach in the living room reading a newspaper he brought with him. Newspapers smell to begin with, and this one probably spent some time in the bathroom. Coach drops the paper and greets you.

"You look good," he says, drawing you to him.

"I better had," you say with an Irish lilt, and return the embrace.

He holds you, and comfortable with silence between kisses, you feel safe. The specter of Zoltán cannot haunt you tonight. The blue bullet does its work. Coach fumbles with the buttons on your nightgown and you turn on your stomach to make it easier for him.

He kisses the back of your neck. You roll over again and meet his eyes, losing yourself.

Chapter Two
Friday, October 30
8:22 pm

You're drunk. The past week has been good; you didn't want to drink. You did anyway. Zoltán often pops into your head; your face burns and your brain spins. The conversation with your father did not reassure you. You want to broadcast your sins to the world to make sure everyone knows how ashamed you are, how bad you feel.

Must confess.

You'll find that priest and spill your guts.

Now you're squirrely, and have plenty of hoo-hah in the kitchen cabinet. After a few shots, you're spacey and gaze out the window to the deck. The pumpkins in the corner entice you into carving one. Jefferson follows you outside and curls up in the opposite corner.

You make a pencil sketch on the best side of the pumpkin, a leering face with giant, uneven teeth, a small, gnarled nose and disproportionate eyes. You hum as you carve, something from *Tosca.* That Puccini guy can sure write a melody.

The neighbor's walnut tree looms, stretching a branch over the deck; a walnut falls and thunks on the boards nearby. You drop the knife and squeal. A gash on your middle finger drips blood onto your clothes. Jeffrey raises his head but isn't concerned.

Shit.

The finger bleeds and you do your best to stop it with a cloth. You race to the bathroom and clean the wound, wrapping it in bandages. The mirror scares you. Like whistling in the dark, you hold your hand up and have a good look at your shoddy first-aid. The finger is huge in its wrapping and you cackle. You're still laughing when the phone rings.

"Hi, Dad."

"Guess what?"

"You're playing the *Emperor Concerto* with the Vienna Phil tomorrow evening."

"Close. No cigar."

"I can't imagine," you say as you yawn.

"I've got two tickets to *Lulu*—early December—at the Met."

This news gives you pep. "Fabulous. Don't you want to take Dennis?"

"No, I want to go with you. It's your favorite."

You're teary but manage to say, "Thanks, Dad."

Silence.

"Ally? Are you still worrying about that other business?"

"Um, no. I'm okay," you lie. "*Lulu* will be great. We can meet and stay in the city. Want me to make arrangements?"

"Sure. I've been thinking of you, listening to a lot of Brahms lately. I miss you. How about if we come south for once, in time for Christmas Eve?"

"I would love that. Dad," you say, hesitating.

"Yes, Dear?"

"I have to go."

"We'll talk again soon."

"Catch you later."

He hangs up. Once again, you didn't say it. Why is it so hard? He and Mom must have said it to one another. I. Love. You. But you can never get past the I. It's easier with Coach. He taught you that much, but you rarely say it first. You frown at your finger and remember you have to accompany the church service Sunday. How will you get around the keyboard? It'll be like trying to play with a boxing glove on your hand.

Saturday, October 31
11:02 am

You fret about what to wear. Coach likes your black leather slacks, although you wear them a lot. After struggling into a pair of jeans, careful not to aggravate your finger, you stand and look over your shoulder into the mirror. You take off the jeans and find the leather.

After you finish dressing you pause in front of the window in time to see a flock of blackbirds scare the cardinals away. "Fuckerrrrs. Gonna bake you in a pie," you say. The cardinals give you hope, but the blackbirds, gluttons, control the bird feeder. You open the window. "Scram!" The blackbirds scatter.

You consider calling the day off because you feel dirty again. The doorbell rings and you have to answer.

"M-Max."

"What is it, Sweetheart?"

"I can't go. I look a mess and I'm nervous—"

"Shhh. Don't worry, Babe. We're staying over. We can check in first and then go to the game—"

"But I have to be in church tomorrow."

"Well, we don't have to stay over. We'll leave right after the game."

You study him. "Really?" You turn to the piano. "Then I can practice in the morning—if I'm not too tired."

"What time do you have to be at church?"

"Ten." You sniffle, poking at your nose with a tissue. "Okay. Thanks."

Coach puts his arm around your shoulders, then tries to take your hand. "What happened to your finger?"

"Never mind."

1:37 pm

Jefferson jumps into Coach's hatchback and you fill his water bowl. The car is too cold and the chill gnaws at you. Explosions of worry assault your stomach, like bombs detonating.

You agreed to fill in for the church's Minister of Music, Maestro Healey, the next morning. The contrast between his artistry and your mediocrity will stun the congregation. Your piano chops are lacking; you haven't practiced much and have a wounded finger to boot, but will concern yourself with that tomorrow. For now, you try and enjoy the moment.

Coach has tickets waiting at Princeton stadium. His friends have connections. You don't want to meet his friends, already imagining what they'll think of you. Coach assures you they're good people. Everyone is good. That's Coach.

3:22 pm

After Jefferson does his duty and he's settled, you and Coach walk the mile from parked car to stadium. By the time you get there you're overheated and grumpy.

"Just be yourself. They'll love you."

"Okay," you say. You say okay a lot. It's an all-appeasing word. And you say it to reassure yourself that everything will be alright.

"Here we are," Coach says, as you approach your seats.

A couple stands, smiling as Coach steps towards them. Like Coach, they're older, but unlike him they show their age. The man is heavy-set, gray-haired, jolly and attentive to his wife, who has a sweet smile, blond hair, and stands a foot shorter than he does. You wait behind Coach as he talks with the couple.

Has he forgotten to introduce you? On one hand, you feel relief and on the other, you're angry. You are not important. You embarrass him. You are too ugly. You—

"Hey, this is my partner, Alexandra McRaven."

The man offers you his hand. "Hi. I'm Buddy," he says and turns to his wife. "And this is Jen."

Jen shakes your good hand. "Nice to meet you."

Your mind races, and you search for words, forgetting the proper thing to say. Then you recover. "I'm Alex. Thanks for the tickets."

"We're happy you could meet us," Buddy says.

"Alex is a composer," Coach says.

Your face burns. "No, I'm not really—not a real composer, anyway." The choral works you compose and arrangements you make get published, but the truth is, you sold out. You strayed from the world of concert music. Your music is easy for people to learn and perform, nothing innovative or noteworthy.

Coach continues, "Yes, she is."

"That's interesting. I don't think we've ever met a composer," Buddy says.

"I hope the good guys win," you say and point at the football field.

As they nod and agree, you imagine they are as happy as you to change the subject.

Coach leads you to your seat, saying, "You did great." He kisses you on the cheek and you sit, grateful for the isolation of the last seat in the row. This way, Coach can talk with his friends and you can check the score when you want and lean over and participate in the conversation when you must.

9:58 pm

Princeton wins over Cornell forty-seven to twenty-one. Tired from the ordeal of having to be attentive to people you just met you remain quiet on the walk to the car. On the highway, you doze. Once home and Jefferson is fed, you and Coach shower together. You wrap your hand in a plastic cover, and the water comforts you, washing away your grimy paranoia. You respond to Coach's caresses and don't know whether you're hot from the shower or sweaty or excited. And it doesn't matter.

Sunday, November 1
8:51 am

Coach leaves early in the morning. You clean yourself up, change the bandage, and go to the piano, stabbing at the keys, rushing in your effort to get from one measure to the next. You sweat, but only wear underwear as you sit on the piano bench; you have time to get your clothes together before you have to leave.

They're just hymns, and luckily, you injured your left hand and your upper register piano hand is free. You wonder what notes you can leave out, how fast you have to take the tempo so it won't seem like a dirge, and whether you should sing along. If you don't sing the congregation won't either. But if you do, the playing will suffer even more. Multitasking is not your thing. You'll play the top and bottom lines and leave out the inner voices.

Your underthings are damp and you change. Although the first day of November is frigid and windy, you wear a short-sleeved shirt and lightweight pants under an overcoat. The condo is about half a mile from church, and you want to walk, but drive instead so you'll get there a little early.

9:52 am

When you arrive, an acolyte tells you Father Marcus is looking for you and you stay in one place to let Father find you. You stand in a corner of the narthex and watch people walk by, young couples with children in tow, older couples with canes and walkers, a few lethargic teenagers, troopers for coming to church on a day when they might sleep in.

"Alex?" Father says.

"What can I do for you?" You put your left hand behind your back so you won't inadvertently flip Father off.

"Did you prepare an anthem?"

"No."

"Well, looks like most of the choir didn't show up today, anyway."

"I could play and sing a short something," you say.

"That's fine. And please sing the opening chant." He swivels and glides away.

The anthem, the musical selection during the Offertory that varies from week to week, doesn't worry you. You peer in the doorway of the church and see the house is packed. If you played the organ, you could remain hidden up in the choir loft. But you lack that skill, and must use the piano in front of the congregation. You walk down the side aisle and take your place.

The bell chimes and you stand and sing the chant. Your voice is clear and even, magnified by the good acoustics in the church.

You play a short introduction to the opening hymn. It is not even, but tolerable enough. It's time for the congregation to enter; you do not sing and you're frantic because no one sings, so then you have to. When you sing the piano does suffer. The bulbous bandage makes it all worse and you panic, playing faster and lunging at the keyboard, making it harder on yourself.

You pound out an unwanted dissonance and see Father jump, then try to play softer and sing louder. You strike a bass note and hurt your finger, saying "Ouch!" aloud. Suddenly, the hymn is finished and you wonder how you got through it.

After the scripture readings, you gear up for the next one. The hymn Father chose is riddled with flats in the key signature. You hate copiously-flatted keys, preferring sharps. You set a slow tempo in your head and play the intro. Your spirits lift as you make it through without a clunker, and all three verses go smoothly. You stop playing and smile to yourself.

Then you glance up. The congregation stares at you and you look at the hymnal. "Oh!" you say. There's another verse left in the hymn. Blood boils against your skin and you feel redness on your face, but you dive into the final verse and sing. The congregation follows. After, Father reads the Gospel scripture, and you take a seat in the first pew to wait for the sermon.

Your anthem comes off well and you're playing better. You sing the melody and fake the accompaniment, fleshing out the harmonies with your right hand as you provide a one-note rhythmic bass line with your left-hand pointer finger. Sweat drips off your nose as you play and sing. People must notice. You prepare for the final two hymns and think of going home.

11:06 am

You hurry to the car. With a sigh, you back out of the lot and drive down the side street, preparing to make a left turn onto the main road. Tall bushes lining this side of the street impede your view of traffic, so you pull out farther. You see a white pickup truck coming from the right, about to turn onto the street where you wait. The truck comes into your lane and sideswipes your car. The scraping of metal-to-metal floods your ears and you squawk. People behind honk their horns, urging you to move.

After you turn around and you're on the street where you began, you see the truck that hit you. You walk over as a man steps out. It's small beside him. He stands tall, wavy black hair a mass on his head. The pressed khakis and Oxford shirt he wears are crisp and neat, especially alongside his dirty vehicle. He inspects the left side and walks with you to your car.

"Hi. I'm so sorry," you say.

Zoltán?

No.

He runs his fingers along the side of the car where the paint is scraped off and the metal is dented. "I am not sure what has happened," he says, his deep, accented voice like Zoltán's, but hushed, gentle.

You take out your phone. "We can exchange insurance info until the police get here."

"I do not think we need police," he says.

You hesitate and say, "I think we do."

He stays quiet. Then he steps closer to you. You want to back away but stand your ground.

"I think I must know you?" he says.

"I don't think so."

"Perhaps you know my brother?"

Brother!

"No," you say, and watch as he takes a wad of cash out of his pocket.

"Here is five-hundred dollars—all I have. It is good?"

You consider this and squint up at his face, heart beating faster.

Chapter Three
Tuesday, November 3
4:58 pm

Wind ruffles Coach's hair as he throws the baseball to you. You can't help admiring him—attractive with glasses, nerdy but handsome, athletic build, thick blondish-brown hair and unruly eyebrows. As far as you can stretch, you hold the glove out to your side, and try to catch the ball. You miss, and giggle.

"Catch it in front of you," Coach says.

"But it might hit my nose!"

"If you hold the glove in front of your face it'll land in it before it gets to your nose." He laughs.

Sometimes you meet Coach at the park after football practice to sit and read or have a catch. The hardness of the baseball scares you, but you love to throw it, knowing how impressive it is. The ball soars in a giant arc over Coach's head after you release it. You would make a good outfielder or third baseman with your cannon of an arm.

"Hey. Your birthday's coming up. What do you want to do?" you say, jogging to him.

"I've been thinking we could drive up to see my sis—if you want."

"Oh." Your stomach churns.

"What's wrong?"

"They don't like me," you say.

"They don't know you."

"They think I'm an opportunist."

Coach laughs. "That's absurd and you know it."

"It may be absurd, but that's what they think," you say.

"I think your resources tally up stronger than mine."

"Does that make you the opportunist instead?"

"Nobody's an opportunist. It's getting dark. And I have term papers to grade. See you after the game Thursday?" he says.

"Not before?"

"Come stay with me for once—keep me company while I work, but I won't be much fun."

"Maybe I should get something done, too. I've been stuck on my latest project for four days," you say.

Coach walks you to the car. After you settle into the seat, he leans in the window. "You know what I want."

"I know. I just can't—not right now."

"What's the obstacle?"

You take his hand. "I'm not acceptable."

"You're plenty acceptable. My family will come around. They just don't understand why you don't have a job, that's all."

"I do have a job." Your voice is low and quiet.

"I mean something nine to five, where you go and interact with people."

"Okay. Sorry. I'm sorry I'm not normal." You release his hand.

You put the seatbelt on and your hands on the wheel. Coach steps away. You back out of the parking space and turn towards home, watching in the rearview mirror as he walks to his car. Although the condo is nearby, you pull off to the side of the road so you can remove your jacket and wipe fresh sweat and tears from your face with the bottom of your sweatshirt.

6:59 pm

When you get home, you let Jefferson out, forego a shower and put pajamas on. Then you make a pot of coffee. You need to cry but tears won't come and you choose a DVD from your collection. *Now Voyager*, with Bette Davis, will force you to cry. As you hear the music during the opening credits, your body relaxes. The movie is a drama—an ugly duckling story along with a gut-wrenching love affair. This sort of angst appeals to you, and knowing the plot well, your mind turns in on itself.

You think back to Sunday after church and Zoltán's brother, who sideswiped your car. You usually consult Coach about things like this—car problems, financial issues and health concerns, then you had the car fixed yesterday without telling him. The accident was probably your fault. You were harried and did pull too far into the intersection, although you had to so you could see. With your money and the man's fat wad of cash, you paid for the repairs.

His black mane of curly hair and impossible height haunt you. You still hear the low tones of his accented voice and feel his intense, goldish eyes upon you. The conversation you had with him plays over and over in your head.

"If that does not cover the cost, please contact me," he said, giving you a business card. "I will give you more—in fact I can get more tomorrow—"

"That's not necessary. Thank you."

"Please—what is your name?"

You hesitated, but only for a moment. "Alexandra." You're tall, but he was so tall you leaned back to see his face. Mesmerized, you caught yourself and looked away, thinking about Zoltán, and how he didn't seem to have his brother's height. Maybe it was the ponytailed hair.

"Alexandra," Zoltán's brother said, and paused. "A strong name for a strong woman."

You turned back to him. He bowed formally, and then got into his truck. After he left, you examined his card—a name with two words under it, an email address and a phone number.

Sándor.

Spiritual Healer.

You snap out of it and shake your head. How could he be Zoltán's brother and so compelling? On the television, Bette Davis is stuck in the back of a car with Paul Henreid. They enjoy every minute of it, although you know it's fleeting.

The emotional release of tears will not come. You get off the couch, walk to the kitchen and open the cabinet. Behind the dishwashing detergent is the jug of Jack Daniels. You help yourself to some coffee and add a generous amount of whiskey to it.

Hoo-hah.

9:10 pm

Jack gives the coffee a kick, which you enjoy, along with the smooth feeling in your head and the release of tension. As the movie draws to a close, you're able to have your cry. Jefferson gets up, comes over and puts his paw on your knee. "Oh, Sweat-pea." You cry harder, and stroke his fur.

You turn off the television, go to the computer and open iTunes. With a playlist for every mood, you find the one you want—Acute Melancholia. Giggling at yourself, you open the playlist to see what pieces of music you chose for it. Beginning with Gustav Mahler and Allan Pettersson, the list is too heavy and you scroll down and see General Moroseness.

The music begins and you snuggle into the corner of the couch as Gabriel Faure's *Pavane* fills the room; the poignant flute melody drifts over the gentle pulse of pizzicato strings. You feel cozy and warm, but need another cup of whiskey-coffee concoction. You frown at the mug, white with piano keys painted on it, a gift from a student. This time you bring the giant bottle from the kitchen cabinet with you. On the way to the couch you pick up the business card.

After you sit you turn the card over and over in your fingers. The background of it is light green—soothing—the green of water off the Bermuda coastline, the color painted on the walls of mental institutions. There is a border on the edge of the card, the rich, dark green of magnolia leaves. And the name and title—

Sándor.

Spiritual Healer.

—beautiful and promising.

You take a long draw of the jacked-up coffee. It gives you a lift, and you look around for the phone. The number on the card is local; he could be nearby. Memorizing the number, you forage in the cushions for your phone and when you find it, fortify yourself with another gulp and dial.

It rings, goes straight to the message, and a mechanical voice says you have reached the number. You freeze as the prompt beeps and hang up.

Then you doze.

10:32 pm

The opening motive of Beethoven's Fifth Symphony pounds in your head, which hurts. You try and shut the music out, but it persists. You wonder why it stops suddenly, without finishing the rest of the symphony's exposition. Of course—your phone is ringing—your phone! You scramble for it and by the time you get there the caller is gone. You see the number you remember from the card and call it back, breathless and shaky.

"Alexandra." The deep voice is mellow.

"That's not a question," you say.

"No. I thought you might call."

"How could you possibly?"

"I have been wondering if you had enough money to cover the repairs," he says.

"Ah, the repairs. Close enough."

"But in truth, I wondered about you."

"Oh?" you say, hesitating. "Why?"

"You are a strong woman, as I said, but you carry a great weight."

You know that already, and don't want to think about it. "Will you go to the game this week?"

"I am not sure. My brother may be able to attend."

"Your brother."

"Yes. My brother, László's father."

"László, number forty-seven," you say.

"You remember well." He hesitates before speaking again. "You are—not right."

This gives you pause and you raise your voice. "What do you mean, I'm not right?"

"We are seeing that you are not yourself, and the spirits—"

"They don't call them spirits for nothing." Your face burns, heat soaking your pajamas. "And who's we?"

"Myself, and the spirit guides. We—maybe you and I can talk sometime when you are more like yourself?"

"I'm just fine right now. Actually, you have a nice evening. I've got to go."

"Please, I mean no offense. Can you hold for a moment?" he says.

"No. I can't hold. If you want to talk, you have your chance now."

"I just have to get my tea—"

"Your tea can wait." You hear the pot whistling in the background and don't care.

"I will be quick," he says.

"Oh, go play with your tea!"

You flip the phone shut, throw it across the room and pass out on the couch.

Thursday, November 5
8:31 am

Your head reels less than it did this time yesterday, and you're grateful. You drank the rest of the whiskey last evening, but there wasn't much left, having outdone yourself the night before.

You think of Coach, but eager to complete your project, you power up the Mac and open the music notation software.

The phone rings and your heart leaps.

"Hello," you say.

"Alexandra McRaven, please," a gruff voice says.

"Alex, here." You smirk, as you do when you've made a mistake, or done something naughty. "Hi, Sam."

"I'm calling about the arrangement. You're late."

"Oh, yes—nice of you to call personally. I'll send it this morning."

"Make sure you do—today, Alex." Sam stays silent for a moment. "You should come visit."

"I'll be in next month, why?"

"Can we meet for dinner?"

"Sam, I've been seeing someone for two years. You know that. It's serious."

"Is he coming with you, then?" he says.

"No, I'm meeting my father."

"Well, I could join you."

"Thanks, but, no," you say.

"What opera?"

"*Lulu*. It's supposed to be a fabulous production."

"But you won't see me," he says.

"No. That's not a good idea. We were forever ago, and it was weird anyway."

"Weird, you say. I'm disappointed. I was sure it was divine."

"I have work to do."

"Indeed."

"I'm sorry for ending things the way I did. But it was inappropriate."

"Get that arrangement here soon," he says and ends the call.

The music is a Bach chorale, and you're arranging it for three-part chorus. Past deadline, you must send a draft to your publisher. Sam, with whom you spent some time in your thirties, is your primary contact with the company and although you still feel for him, your mid-forties are upon you and it's a struggle to function with even one man.

You dive in, entering the final notes before you edit and polish, a tedious business, but you'll be paid well and will complete the task in a few hours.

Thoughts of Coach play in your brain. He still hasn't called. You haven't called him. Later in the day you'll see him at the game, but think you won't go. He may not want you there.

3:54 pm

You sit in your usual place near the top row of the bleachers and tilt your head towards the sky. Clouds, low and dark, threaten to burst. You glance around and notice Sándor is not among the crowds. That's just as well. Once again, you're ashamed of your behavior, not only for being disrespectful with him on the phone, but also because you were on the phone with him in the first place. You zip your coat up the rest of the way, wishing you had a hat and gloves.

Coach stands on the sidelines and faces the field where both freshman football teams push each other back and forth, uniforms stained with mud from the previous night's rain. *Miserable.* But you couldn't stay away. When you're at odds with Coach you're a wreck.

There's no score through the first two quarters, and at halftime the teams form huddles on opposite sides of the field. It starts drizzling and you consider going to the car. You search the crowd and then beyond to the field where Coach stands bent into the huddle. He'll understand if you don't stay. The rain comes down harder and you step down several rows to the end of the bleachers.

By the time you get to the car it's pouring and you rifle through your pockets, looking for the keys. Sodden hair hangs in your face and your jacket is soaked. Finally, you find the keys in a pocket of your jeans and as you fumble with the lock the rain stops falling. You turn around and see Sándor holding an umbrella over your head.

You frown. "You're a bit late for that. I'm already soaked, and now I've found my keys."

"Yes. The rain has you already. But it is not too late for you."

"What's that supposed to mean?"

"We can help."

"I don't need help, thanks. Look, I'm sorry I was rude on the phone, but we're all square. The car is fine and so am I." You open the door and climb in.

Sándor nods.

Friday, November 6
9:31 pm

You wait. A bowl of fruit sits on the table and you poke at it. Except from afar, you haven't seen Coach since Tuesday. You don't eat or sleep and can't work. The liquor store at the back of the bar and restaurant where you had the encounter with Zoltán beckons. You throw a raincoat over your pajamas, put on a hat, the kind with earflaps and tassels, and make the drive. You don't like bars, especially now, and you have to walk through the bar area past the restaurant to get to the store. You cringe, sweating as you push your way into the crowd.

As you pass through the bar, you glance through a window into the restaurant. In a booth off to the side, Coach sits across from a red-headed woman. You recognize her—an administrator from the hospital where you volunteer. You stop by the bar and poke your head around the corner into the restaurant. From here, you can see they are deep in conversation, focused on one another.

Coach, fetching in a tweed sports jacket and black turtleneck, makes your stomach flutter. But your heart sinks as you study the woman, who wears a simple, expensive looking dress. High heels grace long slender legs crossed in a ladylike manner. You remember from the hospital her eyes are green, complementing thick, red hair—not an orangey-red, but the dark and lustrous tone of mahogany. In the dusk of the restaurant they look sultry. Coach glances your way and you leap out of view. People at the bar stare at your feet, and you remember you still wear your ratty old slippers.

Your mind leaps from anger and indignation, going straight to self-attack. With your hands shaking you stand near the door, peeking around the corner.

You had this coming.

"Can I help you?" a petite woman with bouncy blond hair asks.

"No, thank you." You continue to watch Coach and his date.

"I'm afraid I'll have to ask you to leave." She snaps her gum.

You ignore her and continue spying.

"Ma'am?"

Ma'am? You're not that old. "Alright, you snarky little pixy."

You head for the package store but a burly man escorts you out the back exit instead. Now you have to find another store to get your hoo-hah, thoughts of Coach with another woman swirling in your head.

Chapter Four
Saturday, November 7
10:17 am

The tiles you kneel on are cold and hard. You know the toilet's clean but don't want to touch it so you stand, lean over the bowl and throw up. Dizzy, you see the fish on the wallpaper blur and you rub your eyes. You don't remember getting there but from your position on the floor you see Jefferson sitting behind you, upside-down.

You scramble about, trying to get up. After cleaning and brushing your teeth you get back in bed, and bring a damp washcloth with you. The cloth feels good on your forehead; the ceiling fan rotates, cooling you off.

In the moments it took you to pass by the restaurant last night, you saw how engaged Coach was with that woman. They made a striking couple. You recall red hair hanging to her shoulders. Her face was lovely in the dim light—a high forehead over a small nose, and smiling lips.

She dresses better than you, and although older, looks better as well. You groan and roll over, trying to force sleep to come. Then you have a thought.

Sándor.

The tangled bedclothes make it difficult for you to find the phone, so you tear them off the bed. As you shake them the phone falls to the floor. You sigh, wanting to call Coach, but dial Sándor's number instead.

"Hello?"

"It's Alex, remember?"

"Yes," Sándor says. "Of course."

"You said you could help me."

"Yes."

“You also said I carry a great weight. I trust you’re not talking about my present girth.” Your tone is more flippant than you want.

“I do not believe the danger is imminent. But you must be on guard,” Sándor says.

“What do you mean, on guard?”

“A sickness lives in your heart.”

“Hey. I don’t mean to insult you, but how do you know this? Your business card says spiritual healer. Are you some sort of psychic, too?”

“I call myself healer because my goal is to provide a spiritual cleansing, not to predict the future. Fortune telling can be dangerous. Our thought is that through regression therapy or spiritual reading, we can set the soul on a positive, light-infused path. However, we see things—”

“Here you are with this we business again,” you mutter.

“And we are seeing that you are drinking almost every day.”

This gives you pause. “Uh-huh.”

“Yes. You are a good person, but engage in reckless behavior, which leads to spiritual, and eventual physical, collapse.”

“Okay. So, what do I need to do?” You hear chatter in the background.

“Hush, György,” he says. “I apologize, Alexandra. My friend is rarely quiet.”

“You’re not alone? Don’t you have some sort of confidentiality policy?” you say.

Sándor laughs.

“What’s so funny?”

“Please, do not be alarmed. György is my parrot. He is given to being loquacious.”

“Parrot.”

“Yes, he is magnificent, but has—how do you say—a big mouth.”

You harrumph and flop on the bed, imagining this tall, beautiful man with his hair blowing in the wind and a parrot on his shoulder, maybe even a patch over an eye, standing at the helm of a ship.

"Alexandra?"

"I'm here. Well. Where do you set up shop?"

"I am not on the mainland, but on the island."

With a grunt, you grimace. You hate going over that bridge.

"But I could come to you, if I would not intrude."

"Nope, not at all. How soon?"

"I am free later today and then not until the following week," he says.

"Today," you say.

Today!

"Yes, I can, yes. Come and fix me." Excited, you talk as you tidy the bedroom.

"Fix you?"

"Yes, heal me, or whatever it is you do."

"I see."

You sense something in his tone but can't put your finger on it.

"Alexandra?"

"What?"

He hesitates. "I am grateful to help you. But this is not, as you Americans say, a quickie fix."

"It's quick fix, and I'm a fast learner. Can we just start?"

"Yes. We can make a beginning."

"Great," you say.

He sets up a time and you give him your address, but suspect he knows where you live.

4:58 pm

After spending a couple of hours cleaning, the shower refreshes you. When you finish, you go to the closet. As usual, you find it difficult to choose something to wear. You want to look nice, but not dressy, and you have ultra-casual clothes and dress clothes—not much in between. In the closet, you find a dark blue skirt, long and shimmery. It will go well with a black t-shirt and a gauzy, lightweight scarf circling your neck. Jefferson sighs, watching you dress.

You walk through the apartment and notice dust on the frame around the portrait of your mother. The dust cloth is under the kitchen sink and as you get it you see your stash. With a frown, you ignore it and return to your mother. After you wipe the frame you stand back, inspecting your work and the painting.

Sympathetic brown eyes gaze into yours and a gentle smile reassures you all is well. You shake your head and look away. Your sixteenth birthday was not so sweet; the only revelers at the party were hospice workers, and your mother died a few days after.

You look down at the scars on your wrist. The memories are vague—the final days with your mother, that day God tore her out of your life, and months of hazy, festering emptiness. The scars appeared during those months, a gesture you thought you invented, a line of short, bloody slices up your arm.

The doorbell rings.

You shake off the recollection.

Sándor's an hour early. Wisps of damp hair straggle around your face so you pin it up and race for the door, which swings open, and Coach stands in front of you. You keep your jaw from dropping.

"Hey," he says, and hugs you, but your body's rigid. "What's up? You alright?"

"I wasn't expecting you."

"I'm sorry I didn't call. I was passing by so I stopped."

"Okay," you say.

"Can I come in?"

You don't move but look over your shoulder. "Okay."

"You look nice," he says as he moves past you and into the living room.

"No, I don't. I just finished cleaning."

"Cleaning? Are you having company?"

Your eyes widen. "No." You pretend to rearrange some artificial flowers in a vase, forgetting you only clean extensively when you expect company.

"Mind if I have a seat?" Coach says. He takes his wallet out of his pocket and sets it on the table.

"Nope. But I'm busy today."

"I'll just be a minute," he says, and holds his arms out to you.

You lollygag, bending down along the way to remove imaginary lint off the carpet. When you're within reach he grabs your hand and pulls you, sitting you on his lap. You make yourself comfortable in his arms.

"Mmmm," you murmur, in spite of yourself, and think you might call Sándor and cancel.

"Alex?"

"Yes?" Relaxing even more, your thoughts turn to the last conversation you had with Coach, when you argued. "You know," you say, tilting your face up towards his, "I don't even remember how I felt when I saw you last. We talked, and it didn't go well. But it all seems so silly now."

"Alex—"

"I can be myself with you. Thanks for being the one person I feel at ease with."

"Sweetheart, I'm sorry, but we need to part for a while."

You heard him, but only the words, and not what they meant. "I promise; I'll be ready to commit soon."

"I'm serious. Now I need time. Do you understand?"

"What do you mean you need time?"

"Apart. I need to gain some perspective," he says.

"Is there someone else?" You wiggle out of his arms, knowing it must be that elegant woman who works at the hospital.

He hesitates.

You gasp.

"No, Honey."

"But why, then?" The tears come fast.

He stands and moves your way, but you jump back.

"Like I said, I need time."

"I don't believe you," you say through clenched teeth.

Again, he steps forward, and you hold your hand out and stop him, covering your eyes with your other hand. "You don't want me. You're sick of me, and I missed my chance," you sob.

"I won't take much time. Right now, I need some distance; I hope you'll wait for me."

"Of course. Who else would ever have me?"

"Now, Alex," he says.

"Just go."

"I'll check in soon." He walks past you and out the door.

5:49 pm

On the edge of the couch, you sit and stare at the wall above your mother's portrait and then lean forward, resting your head in your hands. You cried as much as you had time for. Sándor will arrive any minute and you try to focus; thoughts fly from one bad memory to the next and on impulse, you go to your computer. The Catholic church by the high school has a website, and lists the hours the priest holds confession. You'll unload your shame and feel better.

You think of the booze under the sink and consider having a snort, but the doorbell rings. You pause in front of the door, gearing yourself up. The bell rings again and you answer, stifling a giggle. Sándor faces the other way, bent over picking up his keys. You smile because his shirttail is untucked, exposing the beginning of the crack of his behind. He straightens, turns around and smiles back at you.

"Excuse me." He tucks his shirt in his pants and hands you some freshly cut flowers. Jefferson bounds toward him, wagging his tail.

"Curious. Jeffrey doesn't like most people, and it takes him a long time to get used to the people he does like."

"I love dogs. I am early?"

"No, I was just regrouping. Thanks for the flowers."

"What is regrouping?"

"Preparing for your visit," you explain. You lead him to the living room and gesture to the armchair, the one Coach likes, and you falter.

"You are disturbed, Alexandra."

"Please, call me Alex. And I'm fine," you say as you take the artificial flowers out of the vase and throw them behind the chair, replacing them with the real ones Sándor brought.

"Alex." He sits and then stands up again. "I would prefer for us to sit on the floor, facing one another. You feel at ease?"

You nod and get comfy, sitting with your back against the couch. He lowers his great height, and sits cross-legged next to your outstretched legs. You smooth your skirt and wait.

He closes his eyes and remains quiet.

The intimacy of silence addles you, and you break it. "You don't mess around, do you?"

"It is good for us to be still. As I first approached you today the spirits whispered to me. I shall allow them to guide me." Sándor opens his eyes and they pierce yours. "Close your eyes."

You obey. After a while you open your left eye slightly. It's getting dark and you want to turn on a brighter light. Even with Sándor so close, your hackles rise as the foyer light flickers. You squeeze both eyes shut again. He speaks and you shudder.

"Infinite spirit, we ask that you bless us and our reading today, and we ask that only light be present within us, and around us. Nothing negative can enter this space of light, and we ask that we remain open to all the goodness you have to offer, and thank you. Blessed be."

"Blessed be," you say.

"You may ask questions now or along the way if you wish," Sándor says.

Before you have a chance to respond, the doorbell rings again. You both jump up, and you answer the door. Your hands tremble, so you hold them at your sides.

Coach looks beyond you and sees Sándor. "I'm sorry for barging in." His eyes flash your way for an instant. "I forgot my wallet."

Sándor stands next to the table, and Coach doesn't take his eyes off him as he picks up the wallet.

"Please allow me to introduce myself," Sándor says, holding out his hand.

Coach puts the wallet in his pocket, studies Sándor's hand for a second, and then shakes it. "I'm Max."

"I am Sándor, here on business."

Coach raises his eyebrows. "What business?"

You compose yourself and move to them. "Sándor is tutoring me." The tone of your voice is too bright.

"He's tutoring you." A corner of Coach's mouth twitches toward a smile.

"Yes. He's from Hungary."

"And how do you two know each other?"

You pause. "Actually, he—"

"My car collided with Alexandra's car," Sándor says.

You lower your head, swallow, and recover quickly. "Sideswiped. But it's all better now."

"I see," Coach says, draws you to him and kisses you hard on the mouth, leaving your knees weak. "I'll be in touch." He walks past Sándor and out the door.

You sit on the couch, and look up at Sándor. “Even with the chatty parrot, I think we better meet at your place from now on.”

Chapter Five
Saturday, November 7
6:37 pm

"I should not have come here," Sándor says.

"It's okay. He was mad at me anyway."

"He loves you very much."

You sit up. "Really? But he doesn't want me anymore, says he needs time away from me."

"Alexandra," he says, and sits down, patting your knee. "He loves you. It radiates from him. And from you."

"But why is he abandoning me?" You brush his hand away.

"Max also carries a weight. But he does not want you to see it."

"Weight? A burden. That's me," you say. "I'm the burden."

"No. You are not. It is not for you to know the nature of the burden."

You frown. "You know what's going on and you're not telling me."

"I do not know—exactly. But this much is certain. He loves you."

"Then why all the secrecy?"

"Max is a wise man. If he is not telling you something it is for your own good," Sándor says.

"Maybe he doesn't want to hurt me," you say, and spring off the couch. "It's that woman. The woman he was with last night." You pace the length of the couch.

"We are not seeing any woman."

"Well, then, perhaps she hasn't appeared to you and your—team—yet."

"What team?" Sándor says.

"You know, the spirits. You're in cahoots."

Sándor stands. "I do not know about cahoots. But we, myself and the spirits, have a healing gift for you."

"Gift?"

"It is in my truck. I will return."

After he leaves you run to the bathroom and look in the mirror, removing the pins from your hair because they're giving you a headache. Wild around your face, your hair lets you know it's time for your roots to get colored again. With a sigh, you leave the bathroom and head for the kitchen cabinet. The giant bottle of Jack is half full and you don't bother with a glass, swigging from the bottle as much as you can before Sándor returns.

He knocks, but you take your good old time, drinking so much at once your head spins. You remember Coach's kiss, and the memory sends shivers up your thighs. You open the door and see Sándor, who strides past you into the living room. He carries a basin and a bag.

You approach him, stand still and reach up, touching his face.

"Alex, do not do this."

You rest your other hand on his chest.

"Please, now is not the time. And you are afflicted," he says.

"You speak in riddles." You move away, pushing a strand of hair behind your ear.

"It must be this way. And you have the black energy."

"Black energy?"

"Negative entities surround you. You make it worse."

"It's hot in here." You remove your scarf and throw it on the couch, then point at the bag and basin. "What's all that?"

Sándor puts the basin on the floor in front of the couch. "May I fill this with water?"

"You know where the kitchen is."

He talks as he fills the basin. "This treatment will help rid you of negative energy."

You peer in the bag and sniff. "Salt?"

"Yes. Sea salt. Ironically, from the Black Sea. This will eliminate your negative thoughts and anger."

"But I'm not angry."

"Do you have some old towels?"

"Yes." You fetch the towels and put them on the floor next to the basin.

Sándor remains quiet. You allow him to take your shoulders and sit you down on the couch. He kneels before you and gently removes your slippers. He lifts your feet and places them in the basin, and then sprinkles bits of salt around them. "Now, sit up straight and take care your feet are close, but do not touch one another. If your toes touch, obstacles arise and black energy cannot freely escape through the soles of the feet."

"What now?" you say.

"Now we pray together. I will help you."

"I don't pray." That's a lie. You pray, but it's something you do only in private.

"Hush," he whispers, closing his eyes. "Infinite spirit, we ask your blessing upon us, within and around us. God, please bless us with your divine love and light. God, please bless us with your divine love and light." Sándor opens his eyes and looks into yours. "Now, you. God," he begins.

"God, please bless us with your divine love and light. God, please bless us with your divine love and light." You continue chanting the mantra, and belch.

"That is good. The salt water is drawing out the negative energies you have stored in your body."

After fifteen minutes of soaking and praying, Sándor points at the basin and you see the water is murky.

"I will attend to your feet, but first I must flush the water, take the towel with me when I leave and burn it."

"Why do you have to burn it?"

"You see the water is now full of dark impurities. I must dispose of it, and make certain the towel is destroyed," he says.

"All of that came from me?"

"Yes, from the darkness that haunts you," he says, as he dries your feet.

"What can I do about that?"

"I will flush first, take the soiled towel to my truck and then we will talk."

You hear Sándor pour the water and the toilet flushes. Eager for answers, you fidget with your hair until he returns from the parking lot. You sink into the corner of the couch. Once again, the door opens and shuts, and Sándor sits by you.

"How are you feeling?"

"I'm dizzy." You wipe sweat off your brow.

He reaches out, places his hand on your forehead and says, "Rest now." He removes his hand. "We continue these treatments—every day. But you must play your part."

"I don't have time." Your tone is harsh; the alcohol is wearing off and you want more.

"We are feeling you should seek help—for your drinking."

You lower your head and hair falls around your face.

"Alexandra?"

"I'm here." You make eye contact with him again. "You're right, of course, you and your entourage."

"As I said, I will help. You must care for your mind, body, and spirit."

"I'll consider it," you say, and lead him to the door.

Sunday, November 8
11:01 am

Light streaming through the window punishes you. You stretch yourself awake and realize you're not at church. You slept off and on, restless, because you didn't booze it up enough the night before. Church can do without you. The beagle jumps on the bed and paws at the blankets, making a nest for himself. You took him out in the wee morning hours, so you can go back to sleep if you want.

Sleep won't come and you dread the day as you anticipate another session with Sándor. And you wonder if Coach will continue to be a part of your life. Your churning gut sends acid to your throat and you swallow it back down, hoping he's not gone forever.

The week ahead is busier than you'd like. Your commitment at the hospital takes time in your schedule, along with the work you must submit to your publisher. Most recent is the children's choir music you composed, and you remember next Sunday you'll try it out on the children at church.

The phone rings and you ignore it. Your day is free as far as you're concerned. Sándor can wait. You drink all afternoon. Your father calls and you know he'll ask you how you are so you ignore him, too. The next day you finish the whiskey and the following day sleep it off.

Wednesday, November 11
1:36 pm

As you put the finishing touches on your face, the doorbell rings. You know who it is, and take your time. Standing back to admire your work in the mirror, you don your hat and waddle to the door, carrying your shoes. You fling open the door and Sándor takes two steps back.

Laughing, you say, "It's a fetish I have."

"This manner of dress is a fetish?"

"Yes. I like to dress up—like a clown. Sexy, isn't it? Except I can't drive in these shoes."

Sándor reaches out and touches one of your oversized, floppy red shoes. He frowns, then smiles.

"Alexandra, I worried," he says, his face darkening as he hands you the basin and bag of sea salt.

"I was fine. Thanks for bringing the stuff. I'll continue the treatments," you say, taking the things. "Want to come with me?"

"Where can you be going, dressed in such a way?"

"Don't you like my clown clothes?" You spin around for him with your padded yellow pants and billowy green shirt, a clumsy gesture. Makeup stretches a smile across your entire face, your cheeks rosy circles of red, eyes surrounded by a sparkly blue that accentuates them. A top hat with red stringy hair attached sits on your head.

"I am charmed," Sándor says, bows formally, and then reaches out and tweaks your red rubber nose.

"I'm going to my commitment at the hospital. You're welcome to join me."

"I am unable to come, but appreciate the work you are doing. That will also help you."

"I guess," you say, and walk towards your car. "I haven't forgotten about you. I'll be done by five and will call you then."

Sándor follows you to the parking lot and waves as he gets in his truck, watching you back out and drive away.

2:47 pm

You make the usual rounds on various floors, bopping in and out of rooms, laughing and joking with patients of all ages. You had to go through training for this commitment, and since you became a certified Caring Clown Volunteer, you've graced the halls of the hospital with your flamboyant presence every other Wednesday afternoon for several months.

After making rounds, you stop by the coffee shop. With a large coffee in your hand you walk toward the exit and Coach comes in, although he doesn't recognize you, and goes straight to the counter. You turn and watch him; he won't want to see you.

You break into a sweat and fear your makeup will run, so you leave. The car is far away and you shuffle across the lot in your clown shoes, wondering if Coach is there to visit that hospital administrator woman.

You don't want to be a hypocrite. What you've done is much worse. The priest at the Catholic church nearby has office hours this afternoon at four-thirty. If you hurry you can see him, and won't have time to go home and change. Your clown clothes will preserve your anonymity.

The church reminds you of a smaller version of Coventry Cathedral in England. You were there with your parents when you were thirteen and were quite moved by it, the modern structure built alongside the roofless ruin of the old.

You walk in the sanctuary and sit in the back row. The ceiling is high, light-colored wood with white beams crossing at an angle for support and large stained-glass windows on the sides. Near the altar on the south side you see the confessional with its little light glowing on top. Father is in.

You open the door, bunching the bottom of your clown suit beneath you and sit. The panel slides over; you know he's in there, waiting. You memorized a prayer of contrition, which you believe is proper protocol, and begin babbling. "O my God, I am heartily sorry for having offended you and I detest all my sins, because I dread the loss of heaven and the pains of hell. But most of all because I have offended you, my God, who are all good and deserving of all my love. I firmly resolve with the help of your grace, to confess my sins, to do penance and to amend my life. Amen."

The priest is silent and you worry. After a moment, he speaks. "When was your last confession, and what is the nature of your sin?"

"Oh. My last confession was somewhere between 1985 and 1987."

"It's 2015."

"I know. I've been lax," you mumble.

"Then you are a Catholic?"

"It's in my blood." You hear someone outside the confessional. "Father, I have to go."

"Don't be afraid. You can make your confession."

You don't want to. Then words fly out of your mouth. "I slept with someone other than the man I want to marry," you cry. Then you hear voices and panic. As you fumble out the door your oversized shoe gets caught and you trip. You catch yourself before your face hits the floor.

Chapter Six
Wednesday, November 11th
7:26 pm

Although you don't like being a passenger, you allow Sándor to drive. He sits tall in the seat, too tall for this tiny pickup truck. It's well beyond sunset and the headlights of oncoming traffic mesmerize you. Sándor is a cautious driver and doesn't jerk you around when he turns a corner.

"Are you warm enough?" he says.

"Yes, thanks."

"Please adjust the temperature as you like."

You look him over as he drives, amused by his politeness and the way he dresses with pressed khakis and Oxford shirts—preppy—but the thick black hair and bold facial features, not to mention his height, would make him look natural in armor with sword and shield in hand.

He drives over the bridge to the island. "It is ten minutes from here."

"Great," you say.

He makes his way to Atlantic Avenue and because there isn't much traffic this time of year, the drive is easier without having to wait for all the lights. Heading north after passing many side streets, Sándor turns right down one of them, toward the ocean. As you approach the boardwalk, he clicks a remote control attached to the visor above him and makes a sharp left turn. A garage door opens in front of you.

Sándor gets out of the truck first, comes around to your side and opens the door. You grab your backpack and follow him upstairs to an entrance you presume leads into the house. He stands aside on the landing and holds the door, allowing you to enter first. The smell of chlorine is the first thing you notice, and when Sándor turns a light on, you see the pool. Now you know why he asked you to pack your bathing suit. You take a few steps forward and hear a mild echo as he speaks.

"They wanted to demolish this house."

"That would have been a shame because of this alone. I can't wait to see the rest."

Tropical plants and cushioned chairs line the perimeter of the pool area. Stars shine through skylights above you. In one corner of the room you see exercise equipment—a treadmill, elliptical machine and various weight-lifting contraptions. The room is warm and you put your backpack on a chair, taking off your coat. You bend to sniff a bloom on one of the plants, a sense of peace washing over you. Sándor turns toward you.

On impulse, you rush forward and hug him. "How did you come by all of this?" you murmur.

"I inherited it from the woman, Marie, who lived here for many years."

"I bet that's a good story."

"We formed a spiritual connection that began when I lived in France."

"How did you meet?"

"We met at a conference. Do you know the book, *Dialogues avec l'ange*—pardon, *Talking with Angels*?"

"No."

"A woman of Austro-Hungarian descent called Gitta Mallasz and her friends had the supreme spiritual experience of communicating with angels. With help, she eventually transcribed notebooks of instructions they had from angels. I first read her book in the French, but it was later translated into Hungarian."

"You're amazing," you say, feeling dumb.

"I attended the Gitta Mallasz conference in 1988, and met Marie. She is also Hungarian, but came here and married an American, after the Second World War."

"When did you move here?"

"After completing my education is when first I came to America, to visit Marie. Then I went back to Budapest to teach for some years. Upon the death of her husband in 2007, she sent for me to come and care for her."

"I'm sorry, but when did she die?"

"It has been two years since Marie passed onto the next part of her soul's journey."

"Was she ill?" you wonder.

"She was aged and not so vigorous; I cared for her spiritually, and she encouraged me in my gifts."

"Your psychic gifts."

"Yes," Sándor says.

"I have so many questions."

"I will answer, if I am able. You brought the suit for swimming?"

"Yup."

"That is good."

Sándor leads you through another door, up a few stairs and down a hallway. At the second door on the left, he stops. "These are the rooms for when you dress."

"Rooms, plural?" you say as he opens the door.

"Yes. You have sitting room, bedroom, and bathroom. I'll show you the rest of the house first."

He leads you down the hallway to another room and opens the door. "This is where I keep our family treasure." He points to a painting of a blond-haired woman wearing a long, blue dress.

"It's beautiful. The dark background against the lighter blue of her dress is striking. Her eyes are averted and she's drowning in that dress. Is she in mourning?"

"I am not sure. This painting has been in my family for over three-hundred years. The artist was a Hungarian portrait painter who also practiced alchemy."

"Fascinating. Must be worth a lot."

Sándor walks you to your room, through the sitting area and into the bedroom. As you see the bath you hiss your breath in and turn towards Sándor. The light from the moon shines through a skylight and the bathtub is the sort you step down to, sunken in the floor. You love baths. Generally, you take showers, but on certain occasions when you want to relax or get warm, you take baths.

"I will prepare us a tea," he says.

9:48 pm

Sándor leads you to a spacious kitchen with a large island in the middle, pots and pans hanging over it—a chef's dream. He takes the pot off the stove, strains the tea into mugs and hands you one. You move beyond the kitchen to the next room.

A baby grand piano stands on one side; sprawling leather couches and chairs are situated on the other side, and you see a large cage behind them. Then you remember. "Where's the parrot?"

"He is in his room for the night," Sándor says.

"His room?"

"Yes. I have two other suites of rooms, and György makes his home in one of them."

"May I see him?"

"Sometime when you are here during the day. György has a routine and he is settled now. If I wake him he might not be altogether himself."

"Ah," you say, and look toward the windows. The blinds are drawn facing northeast and southwest, and floor-length curtains cover the windows facing the ocean. Sándor pulls the curtains aside and you see a deck that stretches toward the boardwalk, the moonlight reflected on the ocean beyond.

"Shall we take our tea on the deck?"

"Absolutely."

“I have covers to ward off the chill.” He grabs two blankets and pushes the sliding glass doors open.

You make yourself comfortable in a lounge chair facing the ocean. Sándor drapes you with a blanket and hands you a mug. He pulls another lounge next to yours and gets settled, his legs hanging over the end. The evening is mild, although steam rises from your tea. You pull the cover up around your neck.

“I can’t thank you enough.”

“Hush,” Sándor says, “enjoy the moment.”

You try to keep your mind still. The tea is hot and you sip it, careful not to burn your lips. A lone runner on the boardwalk passes the house, heading toward Atlantic City. Except for the occasional sound of traffic in the distance, the night is quiet. After a long while you hear Sándor snoring, and you smile. It occurs to you that some evenings by this time, you’re passed out on the couch—or in bed. Tonight, the tea is enough.

Thursday, November 12
12:07 am

Sweat running down your face wakes you and you shiver as the wind blows. You swing your legs over the side of the lounge, stand, fold the blanket and grab your mug. Sándor is not in his chair. As you walk to the door you see him talking on the phone in the kitchen. The aroma of coffee wafts up your nose, and you look for it so you can fill your mug. Sándor sees you and points at the coffee, picking up the pot. As you approach him, you hear the end of his conversation.

You hold out the cup and he pours coffee as he talks. “Gather your things. Yes,” he says, nodding, “I will arrive in one half an hour.”

He ends the call and turns to you. “I fear our time is finished.”

"It would be great if you would drop me off because I have to let the dog out. What's wrong?"

"I must bring László here."

"Is he okay?" you say.

"He will be well enough. It is his father, my brother, Zoltán." He shakes his head. "The police came to their house and took him away."

You cringe. "How horrible for László."

"Yes. Please, hurry. We will speak more on our way."

You rush down the hall and get your stuff. After a wistful glance at the tub, you meet Sándor in the garage.

"Where do they live?" you ask.

"In a house located to the north of you. First, we must get László. You will have to sit in the middle for the ride."

"That's fine."

The streets are deserted on your way to the bridge and causeway. Sándor drives faster this time. You hug your backpack to your chest and turn your head so you can see him. He furrows his brow, intent upon the road.

"Is there anything I can help with?" you say.

"No. I want to make sure László is safe—before his father returns."

"You said the police have him."

"Yes, but only for a while. His friends will pay the fee, you know, for the bailing."

"Is he dangerous?"

"He will be angry, and László will be in the path of his anger."

"Where's his mother?" you ask.

"She passed many years ago—the drugs killed her."

"Oh, my."

"Zoltán has powerful friends."

"Who are they?"

"Best you should not know."

Sándor pulls into the driveway. A teenage boy, who must have been waiting outside, appears. He carries a bag and walks toward the truck. Sándor gets out and meets him. As they embrace you scoot to the middle of the seat. You feel the thud as the boy throws his bag in the back of the truck and extend your hand as he gets in.

"Hi, László. I'm Alex."

His deep voice is low, subdued. "Hey."

You all remain quiet as Sándor drives you home. When you arrive, Sándor walks you to the door.

He kisses you, on one cheek and then the other. "I regret it ended this way. I will call soon."

You watch him walk to the truck.

Chapter Seven
Friday, November 13
5:32 pm

You close the music notation software and go online to email. You haven't heard from Sándor or Coach. Sándor, you understand. Coach's lack of communication pains you. He was angry even before showing up while Sándor was here. Coach says he needs time apart, but wonders if you'll wait for him—wait for what? You don't know what you'll say but type in his email address and improvise.

When you finish you hover over the send icon with the pointer. Then you read the message over and erase the entire thing. If you were drunk, you'd send it. But you're not, and see that much of the email could be misconstrued. Plus, the style is too flowery.

For the first time since Sándor dropped you off early Thursday morning, you think of your hoo-hah. You don't want to drink and start another draft.

Saturday, November 14
8:02 pm

You stumble over things in your way and tear the cushions off the couch, looking for your phone. Its muffled ringing lets you know it's nearby, but you don't find it in time. "Shit." The couch is the sort that unfolds and becomes a bed, so you look beyond the metalwork and see the phone on the floor underneath. You lie on the floor and reach around until you grasp it, then drag your arm out from under the couch, roll on your back and examine the phone, holding it above you.

Coach.

Breathless, you call back. "Hi."

"Hi, yourself," he says.

"Do you hate me?"

He laughs. "Don't be a goofball."

You smile. "Thanks. I thought you were really mad at me."

"Your Alma Mater beat Princeton this afternoon. I just got home."

"I was hoping Princeton would beat those chauvinistic pig-dogs."

"Now, now."

"It's good to hear your voice," you say.

"I read your email this morning but didn't have time to call."

"And?"

"It was good to hear from you, too. This week is crazy but how about next Saturday?"

"I hope I can wait that long," you say.

"You can do it. How've you been?"

"Like I said, I miss you."

"I've missed you. But that thing I said about waiting for me." Coach becomes quiet.

"What?"

"We'll talk."

"You can't say something like that and expect me not to ask about it."

"Alex, I'm old."

"You're in better shape than I am and you're twenty-five years older! It's disgusting," you laugh.

"Please. I just want you to know, I love you, and always will."

"And I love you—hugely."

"I'll stop by Saturday," he says.

"Looking forward."

Sunday, November 15
9:07 am

You only have ten minutes to rehearse with the children and they cower. You don't want to make any sharp movements for fear of frightening them even more. A little boy runs to his mother and hugs her knees, hiding his face in her skirt. The Sunday school teacher nods with a smile, wan and tired, and you press play on the portable stereo.

The music begins with a short piano introduction and you sing the melody along with the accompaniment when it's time. You keep your tone soft, without using your opera voice, gesturing with your hands when appropriate for the words.

The text you set to music is biblical, from the book of Psalms. *Oh, God, be gracious and bless us, and make your light to shine upon us*. The few words the children must learn repeat, making the song easier for them to digest. The child at his mother's skirt sucks his thumb, peeking out of one eye at you, but the other children smile as they sing, and imitate rays of sun with their arms on the words *light to shine upon us*. After several repeats of the song, they catch on to words and melody. The short rehearsal ends; you pack up your stereo and head for adult choir practice.

Maestro Healey is back from vacation, and as you walk in the choir room he yells at the sopranos, giving you a quick wave as you sit. "No, no, no. That's under the pitch!" he says. He has them sing the section again. In your mind, you say a little prayer for them.

When it's time for the altos to sing, you all get it right away. There are more women than men, and most of the men are basses, singing the lowest male part. Healey sings with the only tenor in the group, conducting from the piano. He carries the tenor lines. No mere tenorino, his voice would fill a large hall.

He turns to the sopranos again. "Those notes aren't right." The sopranos hesitate. "What's wrong now?" he says.

"This is too hard to learn in forty-five minutes," one of the church ladies says.

"That's ridiculous. Hear the line in your head and go right to the notes. Don't flounder around and *find* them with your voice."

"Can we hear it again?" another woman says.

He heaves a sigh, and sings their part again, moving his voice into a falsetto when the vocal line is higher. "Now, you."

They repeat after him and succeed. He has the choir run through the piece again and then you all walk to the church in time for the service. On the way, your phone vibrates. You take it out of your pocket, see your father's number and don't hesitate.

"Dad."

"Ally."

"I'm about to go into church. What's up?"

"Can you come up?"

You pause. "I'll see you for *Lulu*, and then Christmas."

"Not 'til then?"

"I've got a lot going on."

"I see. But couldn't you, just for a few days?"

"What's wrong, Dad?"

"Nothing. I wanted to see you."

"I'll think about it. I have to go now."

He knows you're in church. Why not wait until your FaceTime appointment?

The heat is too intense in the choir loft, which is fine for the congregation below, but up here it stifles you. It's a relief when you march downstairs and sing the anthem in front of everyone.

The sopranos rise to the occasion of performance and the congregation applauds after the choir sings. After the anthem, you decide to go home and don't feel guilty about it, hearing your father's voice. The usher frowns when you approach the exit. Undaunted, you push the door open and trot to the car.

Should you call your father back immediately? You stare at the phone before backing out of the parking space. Sweaty and shaky with your chest heaving from lack of air, you breathe harder and gasp.

You know it will pass, and count backwards from fifty to pass the time. Head awhirl, you can't keep the numbers straight. You pull at your jacket and can't take it off, so you open the windows. The shock of cold on your face refreshes you, your body relaxes, and you start to snap out of it. When you get home, all you're able to do is sleep.

1:01 pm

You hear ringing and wake up, then poke around the blankets for your phone. The recent caller list shows two missed calls; one is from Coach, and the other number is your father's. You return his call first.

Dennis answers. "Alex?"

"Hey, Dennis. How're you?"

"Alex. I'm sorry." He pauses.

"Are you okay? Is it Dad?"

"Oh, Alex—so sorry—he couldn't hold on any longer. He died a few minutes ago."

You can't speak.

"Can you come now?"

"Yes." Your head reels. "How?"

"It was his heart. He fell and didn't get up. I think he knew it was coming."

"Why didn't I know about this?"

"He didn't want to tell you—ordered me not to. I thought of telling you anyway."

You want to scream, but restrain yourself.

"I'm very sorry," Dennis says, with a tightness in his voice.

"Horrible, horrible," you cry.

"Are you able to drive?"

Fear twists your stomach. "Yes. I'll leave right away."

You don't hear any more of what Dennis says and hang up. Tears blind you and the pressure in your head weighs upon your body, dragging it into a slump. You speak with the funeral director and arrange to meet him the following day. With steely resolve, you call Coach.

"Hello?"

"Max."

"You're upset."

"It's Dad."

"What's wrong?"

"He—he's dead."

"What can I do, Sweetheart?"

"You can drive up there with me."

"I want to but can't."

"Why not?" you say, your voice too loud.

"I have to be in school."

"Can't you take a few days off?"

You sob through his silence and he finally says, "Not this time."

"Okay. Okay. Okay—"

"Alex. It is okay. You'll be fine. I can't leave now, too many loose ends—"

"What do you mean?" You can't control your sobs.

His voice becomes harsh. "Can you leave it alone?"

You're quiet and finally say, "I'm sorry."

"Me, too. I love you."

Chapter Eight
Sunday, November 15th
3:27 pm

A sliver of light seeps through murky clouds. Around the airport, smokestacks of industrial parks spike into the sky. You increase speed as you approach the Meadowlands. Fortified with coffee, your mind leaps from topic to topic—your father's nervous tic, the Hudson River, swimming with the fishes. You're angry. But if you were ill, sick and dying, that would be okay. You would allow it to happen—no treatment, no getting better—you'd just slip away. You understand your father's feelings.

Getting through New York is easy; you make it across the George without much traffic. You drive faster while you can before you get too sleepy.

Be careful, Ally.

Dad.

You remember in times of stress his left eye and mouth always twitched. You knew when he was agitated, because his eyes would blink quickly, and you'd see him struggle to hold his mouth still. When you were a child, his face told you when it was time to stop whatever mischief you were up to.

But mostly, you recall him at his desk in the corner of the living room smoking a pipe as he worked, your mother curled up on the couch reading a book. With the exception of music in the background, the house was quiet, and the smell of aromatic tobacco soothed you.

As you pass through Hartford at five-thirty, traffic is not too heavy. You just want to get there but you're still a few hours away. The radio doesn't offer many music choices, but you find NPR and listen, putting the rest of Connecticut and Massachusetts behind. You want to smoke as you do when in the car for extended periods of time. You haven't smoked for almost a year. If you were off the highway you would stop and buy a couple of packs. But you're safe for now, occupied by news segments and interludes of jazz.

When you get into New Hampshire, it's approaching eight o'clock. As you head north, the hills roll under you. Eventually, you see silhouettes of the White Mountains in the distance. You've been to the cabin many times since your father asked Dennis to move in. He gave up his apartment in Durham when he retired and his status changed to professor emeritus, and moved to the summer cabin permanently.

It begins to snow as you pull up the well-lit driveway and park—a few drifting flakes, large and lazy. You get the beagle out of the car and he pulls you towards the woods; he does his duty and you drag him to the cabin. It's muddy and you stomp your boots on the deck, scuffing the rest of the mud off on the doormat. The door opens shortly after you ring the bell.

"Alex. I'm glad you're here," Dennis says, touches your arm, and bends to scratch the beagle behind his ears.

"The drive was easy, but—it's good to see you, Dennis." You hug him.

He takes your bag and leads you into the house. You let Jefferson loose and he explores.

Dennis stops, and the bag falls with a thump. "I can't believe he's—not here."

"I don't think it's registering with me yet." You take his hand and squeeze it. "I need sleep now."

"I understand."

You pick up your bag and move towards the stairway. Jefferson stretches and nuzzles Dennis before he follows you up the stairs.

Monday, November 16
11:52 am

You're trying to sleep and hear the phone ringing. The room is dark but you can tell it's light outside.

"People have been calling all morning. News travels fast. They all love Professor Mac," Dennis says.

"Cormac McRaven. Such a name." You sigh. "Yeah—a loss for everyone."

"I'm still in shock," Dennis says, but when he hugs you again, the thin frame of his body shakes in your arms.

"Me, too."

"Have a seat while I check on lunch," he says, leading you to the living room.

You gaze out the large window into the woods and watch the snow fall, recalling a time a few years back when you visited your father. He sat at the piano; a tumbler of Scotch rested on a table next to it. You sat next to him and grasped your mug, Van Gogh's *Starry Night* printed on it. You played four-hand piano arrangements of Beethoven Symphonies that night, sipping your drinks.

"I'm so bad at this. Can't we just sing?"

"It's good for what ails you," he said.

You grumbled under your breath and took a bigger drink of Scotch than you wanted. Throughout the evening, you played the game. Neither one of you mentioned it, but you knew you were playing. You were supposed to sip and try to make the Scotch last, but your father always outlasted you.

"Why do I have to play primo? Ugh! At least with the bass part I can just bang away. This allegro is killing me."

"You're doing fine. Remember, slow and steady wins the race."

"That's just grand but we're not tortoises."

He laughed.

You eventually got up with a grunt and collapsed in an armchair.

After another drink, you read through songs of Robert Schumann—songs of a poet's love. They are from a man's perspective but you loved to sing them. Certain songs made you weep, and you didn't make it through the cycle.

"Ally, it's time to say goodnight. You know you become overwrought when you're tired."

"Mom would sing these much better. How she loved her Schumann. Mom—" you cried, drunk and sloppy.

"Hush. You sing beautifully, a different interpretation, darker, but beautiful still."

He put his arm around your shoulders, encouraged you to go to sleep.

The sound of Dennis's voice snaps you out of it. "I made chili—been slow-cooking for hours. Is that good for you or do you want something lighter?"

"Chili sounds great for a cold day. Thanks." You help him set the table and take a seat opposite. "The meeting with the funeral director is this afternoon at three."

"That'll give us time to eat and clean up."

"I hate to ask, but do you have anything to drink?" you say.

"There's a case of wine in the basement. We got rid of all the alcohol in the house but someone sent the wine the other day."

"Sorry, but no thanks. Wine makes me sick."

He pauses. "I'm sorry for your loss, Alex."

"And I'm sorry for yours. He loved you."

"I know. But you more than anything." He hesitates. "I always worried you resented me."

"When you came along a few years back it was good for him."

"He worried about you."

"He did?" you say.

"All the time. He said you drank like he did—with some semblance of dignity—but too much. Then he would give me this sad smile."

"Yeah, well, yes. I get my work done, and still have energy left to do a little real composing. That's all I need."

"Drinking weakened his heart and it couldn't take any more."

You wait for him to continue.

"He was going to ask you to get help next time he saw you."

You sigh. "I've been hearing that a lot recently."

"He thought it was too late for himself, and couldn't stop."

Your chili is cold and you add more sour cream anyway then mix it in with some cheese. The result turns your stomach and you slide your chair back. "I have to lie down for a while."

"That's a good idea," he says.

"Please leave the dishes. I'll do them before we go."

3:35 pm

You shudder—your father's corpse lies stretched out in front of you. He wears a suit with an outrageous, wide tie—royal blue with green and orange flowers—and green high-top sneakers, and in his left hand, his finest meerschaum pipe. You glance over your shoulder at Dennis, frowning. "What's with the tie—and the shoes?"

"His wishes," he says quietly. "He wants you to know his sense of humor remains intact."

"I get the point."

You sit with Dennis and visit with your father for the last time. It didn't take long to go over the arrangements with the funeral director. Your father's cremation service will take place the next morning. St. John's Episcopal Church in Portsmouth will host the memorial service a week from Saturday, with musicians and speakers. Your father had that arranged already, and you have time to notify friends and relatives.

"When do we meet with the lawyer?"

"That's Friday morning," Dennis says. You and your father spoke last year and decided you and Dennis would be co-executors of his will.

"How are his finances?"

"You know how scattered he was with practical stuff. I took over his bills a long time ago. Everything's in good shape."

"Thanks. Do you think you want to stay?"

"It won't be the same. But I'll stay. I hope you'll visit," he says.

You sigh. "Seeing all of his stuff makes me miserable. We'll have to go through it. I'll have the piano moved to my condo. What do you think?"

"I like that you want the piano," Dennis says.

"And I like that you want to stay."

Dennis takes your hand. "Thanks."

"Thank you for caring for him."

On the way home from Portsmouth you stop at the grocery store. While Dennis waits in the car, you push your shopping cart through the store and gather three cases of cheap beer. You want to get drunk, not savor the taste. As an afterthought, you throw in a couple packs of fine beer for Dennis, just to be polite.

Tuesday, November 17
10:12 am

It's over, your father's body consumed. You sweat and think of the words...*and He is like a refiner's fire.* These words from the aria within Handel's *Messiah*, "But Who May Abide the Day of His Coming," run through your head now. You think of your father burning up in the furnace temperatures of the crematory. He was a drinker, but his fierce love of God and positive outlook kept him sane. You don't know what to believe, and although you want to, the story—Christ's birth, life, crucifixion and resurrection—is way too good to be true.

And who shall stand when He appeareth. For He is like a refiner's fire. The aria ends, fiery and dramatic. Your concept of God is hazy, and the thought that it is all true scares you. In the end, you might burn up like your father just did, but not in a crematory. You're going to—

"Alex?"

"I'm sorry. I was daydreaming." Hung over and irritated, you don't want to snap at Dennis. "I'm glad you're here with me for all of this."

"I feel the same. Today is—harder. Do you need anything while we're in town?"

"No. Let's just get back."

You remain silent for a while. As the car climbs into the mountains, your spirits lift a bit. "Dennis, I had a look at the instructions for the memorial service. The speakers all have different tasks assigned—poems, scripture readings, music and even some jokes. There's a place for me in the schedule but Dad didn't give me anything to do."

"I was going to talk to you about that. He said you would come up with something."

"Great," you say with a huff. "I don't think I'll be able to sing. I don't know what I would say, and have nothing to read."

"What have you been writing lately?" he asks.

"I just finished another children's piece for my anthology. Other than that, my big project is a pipedream."

"How so?"

"Years ago, I wrote a mass, and for the last two years I've actually been working on a requiem."

"That's tremendous. Can you use anything from it for the service? There are plenty of musicians around."

"It never occurred to me. I'll see what I can come up with."

For the rest of the way home themes from *Carmen* run through your mind. You've sung *Carmen* in concert, and you think of the famous *Habanera*. The rhythm of the dance persists, not soft and sultry like in the opera, but pounding in your head full-tilt. BUM…bah DUM-dum. The force of the rhythm placates you, and your thoughts take a turn. *Lamb of God, you take away the sins of the world, have mercy on us*.

If only.

Thursday, November 19
2:47 am

Tuesday, you switch from beer to coffee, and only leave the piano to sleep and eat. BUM…bah DUM-dum. The habanera rhythm loops in your head, your left hand playing it while your right hand improvises, trying to find the proper notes. You stop every so often to write more down. Usually, you compose directly from your mind to the computer. But now you like the feeling of the keys under your fingers, the pulse of the rhythm and the way the right-hand music snarls over it. While the left hand keeps the beat, the right hand stays busy, and the vocal line is straight-forward.

The few words you have to set for the *Agnus Dei* repeat and you have the melody in your head already. You could almost accompany yourself, and with practice, you think you might try it for the service rather than getting someone else involved with playing for you. *Dona eis requiem, sempiternam*. Grant them eternal rest. You repeat the word *sempiternam* as the habanera rhythm gets softer, the right-hand figures dwindling, while your voice sustains the Latin word for eternal.

Your father would approve, enjoying the juxtaposition of the somber text over the swirling, atonal right hand and the dance rhythm in the left. Yes, you'll be a one-man show for the memorial service—should be a hit.

Friday, November 20
10:07 am

You and Dennis sit in the office, across the desk from your father's lawyer. You have a few questions about your father's will regarding the role of the university as the possible beneficiary of a large sum of money. He narrows his eyes at Dennis. "As you see, you're entitled to the cabin and its surrounding property." The lawyer's hawkish nose points your way and you notice his eyes are too close together. He is efficient and brief. You don't like him.

"We know that," you say.

"The contents of the cabin go to Mr. Dennis Krause, with the exception of the piano, a Steinway Model M. That goes to Ms. McRaven."

"I prefer Miss," you say.

"Excuse me?"

"Miss. We're bludgeoned with feminism enough already. Miss McRaven." You scoot your chair closer to Dennis.

"The inventory of your father's possessions includes a collection of signatures by famous composers," the lawyer says.

The signatures, precious to you, are individually framed, and also include a painting or photograph of each composer.

He continues. "If you choose not to keep them they go to the University of New Hampshire, and you'll receive the money instead."

Dennis says, "Alex wants those."

"That is up to her," the lawyer says.

"Yes, I'll take them."

"Of course. They're quite valuable."

Sunday, November 22
11:31 am

"Happy Birthday," you chirp, and hold the phone away from your face so Coach won't hear your sniffles.

"Thanks, Sweetheart. How's it going?"

"The cabin feels hollow without Dad. We've been busy. Dennis had all of Dad's finances in order so we took inventory of everything valuable. Now we're making preparations for the memorial."

"Sounds like a lot of work," Coach says.

"It's not bad. Really, we just have to organize some things here in the cabin—books and music, the signatures—that sort of thing. Dad's latest book will be published posthumously. Dennis is finishing the final edits and the university press will accept it, I'm sure."

"How're you?"

"I'm—hanging in. I hope I didn't upset you too much before I left."

"I was just tired. Sorry for blowing up. I wanted to drive up with you, but it didn't work this time. I love you."

"I love you, too. How's football?"

"It rained Thursday and the field was muddy. The kids love the mud."

"What're you doing for your birthday?"

Coach pauses.

"Huh?"

"I was thinking. I'm not sure. I wanted to drive up and see Joanie, three hours up, three hours there and three back. They're not answering when I call."

"I'm sorry. I hope you won't be alone today."

"It doesn't matter. When's the memorial service?"

"Saturday morning at ten. It's going to be long. I dread it."

"You'll have a lot of support; both you and Dennis need it now. I wish I could help but I want to see you when you come home."

"Thanks. I need you, Max."

"Same here. Please check in again soon."

"I will."

Chapter Nine
Saturday, November 28
10:02 am

You sit with Dennis in the front row of pews in St. John's Episcopal Church listening to *Terpsichore*, instrumental dances composed by Michael Praetorius. The ensemble playing is situated in front of you. The music makes you smile because you think of geese honking, the jaunty rhythms of this movement accentuated by sackbuts, early versions of trombones, other original wind instruments and organ.

People still file into the church and have trouble finding seats. Many stand in the back as the musicians in front finish and the organist plays a solo work by J.S. Bach, the *St. Anne Prelude and Fugue*. The rector of St. John's approaches and you stand.

"Good morning, Father Wilder."

"Hello, Alex, Dennis. I think we should begin. The church's capacity is almost full. Do you feel ready?"

"As ready as we can be," Dennis says and looks at you.

You nod. "Thanks for everything."

"You're very welcome, Dear."

The dean of the university's school of music walks to the podium, clears his throat and reads a short verse from a poem by Sarah Williams:

> Though my soul may set in darkness, it will rise in perfect light;
> I have loved the stars too fondly to be fearful of the night.

The dean sits and a tall woman dressed in an electric blue dress walks in with a small man wearing a black suit with a blue shirt that matches her outfit. She stands in front of the audience, solemn and quiet. You hold your breath, waiting for her to begin, wondering how she'll find her note, because she must sing before the piano plays. Like you, she's a mezzo-soprano, and when she does sing, her voice, although lighter and more lyrical than yours, fills the church. She must have perfect pitch because she nails her opening notes and the piano rushes in. "Pass me by, pass me by!" she sings in German, frantic and terse.

You know the song well. There are two speakers in Schubert's *Death and the Maiden*. The maiden pleads for death to leave her alone, because she is still young. However, death asks her to take his hand, and she will sleep quietly in his arms. In the song, death offers comfort and relief. As the piano plays the softly pulsing final chords you relax into your seat and take a deep breath.

The people in the church remain still. The pianist begins the second song, and the woman, with a triumphant smile, sings *Going to Heaven*, a short song by Aaron Copland. The music is sprightly, fast-paced and optimistic in tone. The audience claps with vigor when they finish. As they exit Father Wilder stands in front. He extends his arms and recites a few verses:

Blessed are those who mourn,
for they shall be comforted.
So do not fear…

A string quartet of faculty members of the university called the *Epic Quartet* positions in front. They play a movement from two different string quartets, the first by Beethoven. Your father chose the short movement from Beethoven's *Op. 130, String Quartet No. 13*. At first you think his choice is odd because of the brevity of this second movement, marked *Presto*. Then, you get it. The movement passes with constant energy, rapid and fleeting.

The second selection is the first movement of a string quartet by Jean Sibelius, written before his Fourth Symphony. There are echoes of the symphonies and tone poems in this quartet, subtitled, "Intimate Voices." You know most of the music for the memorial service, but poked around in your father's library last week and did some research. Sibelius wrote in a letter to his wife that this piece is the "kind of thing that brings a smile to your lips at the hour of death."

After the string quartet movements, your father's administrative assistant stands and moves to the podium. She is a petite, iron-haired woman, dressed in sturdy black shoes, a green pencil skirt and black blouse. She reads two poems, beginning with Alfred, Lord Tennyson's *The Kraken*. She lifts her face, streaked with tears, and reads the final lines:

Then once by men and angels to be seen,
in roaring he shall rise and on the surface die.

During the poem called *The Dance*, by William Carlos Williams, the audience laughs a bit as she smiles and reads:

Kicking and rolling about the Fair Grounds,
swinging their butts…prance as they dance.

The words conjure up images in your head that make you smile as well, and you think you might get through this day.

The centerpiece of the memorial service floods the hall—the joyous strains of the opening of *Octet in E-flat Major,* for strings, by Felix Mendelssohn. Your mind wanders and the music makes you think of the Strauss tone poem, *Ein Heldenleben*, also in E-flat Major. A Hero's Life. A hero's key, just like Beethoven's *Eroica*. The Mendelssohn is a perfect choice.

The first movement of the octet ends and a professor from the university, another dear friend of your father's, Professor Dunn, shuffles to the podium; his suit jacket hangs off him and his tie is too long for his short torso. In contrast to his stooped frame, his stentorian voice booms through the church as he reads one of John

Donne's *Holy Sonnets*, "Death Be Not Proud."

The silence of audience and lack of sounds from outside disturb you. You listen, and think of how you tried to set Donne's sonnets to music once, and were unable to capture them. Maybe you were too young at the time, but now, here in the quiet church with the speaker's booming voice you feel music course through your veins:

One short sleep past,
we wake eternally and death shall be no more;
Death, thou shalt die.

After a long pause, people in the congregation shift in their seats, blow noses and cough. Professor Dunn moves to the next reading. It's short, and even as tears well up in your eyes, you smile. Your father's choices for the ceremony, both readings and music, haven't failed to engage the audience, and the few words from a stanza by Emily Dickinson bring hope:

Thank God there is a world and that the friends we love
dwell forever and ever in a house above.

After solo piano works by Claude Debussy and Maurice Ravel, it's your turn. You bite your tongue, trying to get some moisture in your mouth. It doesn't work. Parched, you lick your lips. The piano looms, and you take your time getting there. As you sit and smooth your black Maxi dress under you, the word Maxi repeats in your mind—the name makes you cringe, and you think of feminine products, but that's what it's called and you bear it.

You pause with your left hand hovering over the keys below middle C. Then you begin. Bum…bah-DUM-dum, Bum…bah-DUM-dum. The right hand enters over the habanera rhythm in the left, and after the flourishes in the upper register of the piano settle, you sing. *Agnus Dei qui tollis pecata mundi.* The first statement of the text comes easily, and you focus on your playing, barely noticing the huge sound of your own voice.

After the second repetition of the text you move on to *Dona eis requiem, sempiternam*, in the end, repeating the word "sempiternam." The right hand disappears from the texture and leaves the audience with the habanera rhythm, this time using notes that are brighter than the initial appearance of it, reinforcing the Latin word for "eternal." Suddenly, you finish and sit still, listening to the quiet of the church.

You stand and face everyone—stuck in the glare coming from above you. The people burst into applause; you don't know what to do with that and try to compose yourself. Instead of bowing, you nod your head slightly and look at Dennis, whose smile encourages you. Applause still thunders through the church; you think of your father and the giant crowd here to celebrate his life.

You can't help it; your eyes fill, and tears drip down your face, off your nose and chin. With your face in your hands, you remain in front. You can't tell if the church is quiet yet but your impression is that of heaviness, like you're muffled with a shroud.

11:51 am

Dennis is the final speaker for the service. He reads the last section from Walt Whitman's *When Lilacs Last in the Dooryard Bloom'd.* His voice, mellow and steady, grounds you, although you drift in and out of awareness. Dennis' voice breaks, *Passing the visions, passing the night.* The night will be long for both you and Dennis for a while. *I cease from my song for thee.*

Your father loved Whitman and he loved Hindemith, who set this text to music. You don't get Hindemith, but respect your father's regard for him. *With the lustrous and drooping star with the countenance full of woe.* You imagine everyone who knew him, and even the universe beyond, weep for your father. *For the sweetest, wisest soul of all my days*. The words hit you, and tears flow again—your father's love for art, all people and his gentle prodding for you to see the best in everything, do what's right, allowing God to care for you. *And for his dear sake, Lilac and star and bird twined with the chant of my soul*. You lower your head.

Dennis finishes and the organist begins to play a piece by Olivier Messiaen. The music creeps in, quiet, spacious and eerie, the *Celestial Banquet*. There are other pieces for organ your father could have chosen, but this piece sounds like a transition from this world to the next, the audience transported to the reception after the service as your father moves from earth and takes his place at the Heavenly Feast.

You and Dennis rise first, walk toward the church's entrance and then stand and wait to greet everyone as they depart. People file past slowly, and although most of them only know Dennis, they speak to you as well, with hugs, sympathies and compliments on your music and singing. You brighten and finally the end of the line is in sight. A member of the university's voice faculty talks to you.

"The *Agnus Dei* is stunning. I'd love to hear the rest of it. Has the entire requiem had a performance?"

"Not yet. I haven't sent it anywhere."

"Here's my card. Please give me a shout and we'll talk." She leaves and as you turn back to the line someone takes your hand. A flood of feelings, from surprise to concern, from elation to caution, scurry around in your stomach.

"Max." You sigh, and hug him.

"Hi, Sweetheart," Coach whispers in your ear as you embrace. "Great job."

Chapter Ten
Saturday, November 28th
3:27 pm

Settled in Coach's hotel room, you want to frolic but you're both too tired. There are too many issues to address before you rest, and your clogged brain won't function. Dread in the pit of your gut nags at you. Still, you don't want to talk. Curled up in Coach's arms, his gentle snoring lulls you to sleep.

7:58 pm

Room service arrives—prime rib with a pot of coffee. You put the two trays on the bed and try to enjoy the meal without talking. Then you can't help it.

"What's going on?"

He puts his fork down and takes your hand. "I don't have long, Honey."

"You don't have long."

"I have lung cancer, and there are no treatment options. It's advanced—inoperable."

You move his hand to your lips, and whisper, "Not you, too."

He draws you to him. "Alex." He buries his face in your hair, inhaling deeply. "You'll be fine. Things have a way of working out."

"I should've said yes a long time ago. I wanted to, but never felt like I was—was good enough."

"That was never the case. I love you."

"I love you, too," you sniffle. "I'm so stupid. Stupid, stupid, stupid." Sobs strangle your throat and you can't speak.

He reaches out again, and you let him rock you back and forth until you calm down.

"Why didn't you tell me?"

"There was never a good time, and then your father—"

"When did you find out?" you say.

"November Second, to be exact. I wasn't feeling well for a while—tired all the time—and then I finally checked on it."

"Did you tell your family?"

"Yes. I drove up on my birthday," he says.

"You never smoked or did anything bad for you. And you have lung cancer."

"I'm sorry, Alex."

Tears and nose flowing, you hide your face in your hands. Coach lets you cry and then holds you again.

You recover and lean out of his arms. "I never even asked how you're doing with all of this."

Coach smiles, his lips parting, and he looks down. "I think I'm handling this better than most, friends or family."

"I wish I had known, then I might have behaved better," you say.

"It is what it is, and you did the best you could. There's one woman I spoke to for support a couple of times, a breast cancer survivor, and she helped me."

You can't help yourself. Jealousy flares up in your stomach. "How so?"

"We talked about you, too."

"Me?"

"Yep. She suggested I be as present as I could to you, and tell you when I absolutely had to. I bragged about you quite a bit."

"What the hell for?" You understand now, but the idea of her still irritates you.

C'mon, you dumb-ass. Don't be a fool.

"You're a good person, beautiful inside and out, and the most frustrating thing about you is you don't believe that."

"Oh, Max." You hug him, cry some more and kiss him.

He responds with energy at first, then draws back. "I want

to make love to you, but I'm afraid it won't work."

"I just want kisses."

Sunday, November 29th
7:16 am

Traffic isn't bad when you drop Coach off at the airport and start back to the cabin. You'll head south tomorrow, eager to get home to Coach. He wants you to keep up with your schedule and honor your commitments, and you want to spend time with him. He'll be with his family a lot, but you want to be a part of things.

You've been good about not drinking since you composed *Agnus*, and there isn't time to revel in slosh now.

When Dennis opens the door of the cabin Jefferson runs to greet you, barking and whimpering, wondering where you've been. "Hi, Sweet." You crouch and hug him. "Thanks for taking care of the wee beastie," you say as you stand and embrace Dennis.

"Last week Max called, said he was flying up and would take a cab to his hotel. We had a plan and I'm glad it worked out. Good he made the service and was there for you."

You cry and tell Dennis everything. "So, I have to leave right away. There's a glitch because I have these tickets to see *Lulu* Thursday evening, and Dad—" You fight back tears and swallow hard. "Dad and I were going to go, and now I'll have to go myself or find someone else. Do you want to go?"

"I'm sorry, Alex. I have to get back to work this week. It's time."

"Okay. I just wanted to ask."

"Thanks," he says.

"I'll probably leave in the morning when you're still asleep. If I get settled early I can get up at three and go."

"Good idea. I was wondering, you and your dad video chatted Sunday evenings. Would you like to continue the tradition and meet me once a week, just to check in?"

You take Dennis's hand and hug him again. "I would love that—great. You don't have to wait for Sunday evenings, either. Thanks, Dennis."

Monday, November 30th
2:21 pm

The beagle is quick about his business when you get home and you're tired, unsure what to do. Thoughts of Coach ran through your mind all the way home, and now you have to call.

"I'm home," you say when he answers.

"Good, Sweetheart. How was the drive?"

"Not bad. I missed a lot of traffic leaving early and only had to stop for Jefferson twice."

"What's on your mind?"

"I want to spend time with you. But I've got this thing in New York Thursday evening. I guess you can't go with me, huh."

"No, Joanie's down for the week."

"Yeah, that's good. I'll cancel my plans."

"Alex, you should go. Remember, I want you keep things normal. It'll be good for you, and with Joanie here you can't spend every minute with me."

"Are you sure?"

"Absolutely. You sound tired," he says.

"Yes. I'll unpack and go from there. Can I come over in the morning?"

"Yup. I'll even make breakfast."

"You?"

"I'm not helpless, you know. I love you."

"I love you, too."

9:02 pm

You're groggy from sleep, so you can't find your phone. It's ringing and stops before you find it in the kitchen. You see who called and ring back immediately.

"Alexandra," Sándor says.

"Hi."

"How are you feeling?"

"Not so good. But I have a favor to ask."

"What is it?"

"I know you have clients and a parrot to care for, but is there any way you would go to New York with me Thursday evening? I have great seats for the opera."

"I can leave György in his room for a night. I love the opera."

"Great. That's one worry eliminated. I'm not up to going by myself."

"You should not go alone, true. I am honored to attend."

Tuesday, December 1st
11:12 am

Coach makes an odd breakfast—eggs sautéed with spinach, a bit of Swiss cheese with a touch of cayenne pepper, and steak with spicy mustard and horseradish. You're reluctant to eat in front of his sister, and watch Coach bustle around the kitchen from where you sit.

"Come and have something," Joanie says.

Coach pops a piece of bread in the toaster. "I'm almost done. Anyone need anything while I'm up?"

"No, we're fine. Sit down and enjoy your cooking."

He takes a seat next to Joanie, across from you. "Thanks, Sis, but I really can't eat much these days."

The room grows quiet.

Joanie puts her fork down and her arm around Coach's shoulder. He doesn't pull away, but shakes his head. "I just want some sense of normalcy."

"This isn't normal," you say under your breath.

"He's right. I'm famished," Joanie says and stabs her steak.

You can't move, and don't want to cave in and cry.

"Alex?" Coach says.

"It looks delicious, it really does, but I can't eat right now," you murmur. You stand before you start crying. "It's nice to see you Joanie. I'm sorry, I have to go."

Coach walks you to the door, and then you cry. "I'm sorry."

"It's alright, don't worry. I'll stop by later." He kisses your cheek and you leave.

11:38 pm

You've been sleeping and wake with a start, as Jefferson barks. This alarms you because he's usually too lazy to get up and check things out. You find him at the front door looking out the window. "What's wrong, Jeffrey?" He sees you and barks again until you shush him. "There's nothing there, you mouthy little thing." But a shadowed vehicle pulls out of the lot, with no headlights. Jefferson continues to sit in front of the window, a low growl in his throat as you go back to bed.

Chapter Eleven
Thursday, December 3rd
1:28 pm

After you drop the beagle off at the kennel, you hurry over the bridge. You want to get to the city ahead of rush hour. Sándor closes the garage door as you arrive, and when he switches his backpack from one shoulder to the other he sees something down the street. You follow his gaze.

A large, black car trimmed in gold drives slowly toward Sándor's house. Sándor glances at you and walks toward the approaching car, standing in front of it until it stops. He hurries to the back window. You hear heated words from Sándor and laughter from the car. You're curious so you approach.

Zoltán steps out of the car and says, "Well, here we all are." He starts to walk around Sándor to you.

Your stomach flips; you back away.

Stubbled with coarse hair, Zoltán's face makes your mind lurch to childhood years and your cousin, his legs crawling with hair, his scratchy beard against your face.

As you shudder, Sándor takes your arm and moves towards your car, away from Zoltán. "We have to leave now; we will not be on time."

"And where can you be going—evening dress in the afternoon?"

"Please go, my brother," Sándor says.

Zoltán laughs again. "Will you not introduce me? It is not like my polite and gracious brother Sándor to neglect his manners."

Your mouth runs dry but you manage to pipe up, "I'm just a friend. Nice to meet you, but we do have to go."

"Come," Sándor says, and you walk with him to your car. After you get in, you watch as the black car backs down the street, makes a three-point turn and drives away.

"You know my brother."

"Yes." Your face burns.

"I was aware of it. He asks questions. And I feel his connection with you."

"Connection?"

"My brother—has the gift—the knowing—as well. But his gift is not—bridled. He uses it with anger and for bad things."

"What makes you think I know Zoltán?"

"I sensed you. Not only do we have a gift, but we are twins. Even without the knowing, I might still be able to feel you through the intimacy you had with Zoltán."

"It wasn't a good experience."

"Perhaps not, but now you must be careful. He is restless and will also want you because you are connected to me."

You feel Sándor's eyes but keep yours on the road.

4:52 pm

You're stuck in the Lincoln Tunnel; time passes as you listen to music. Alban Berg's *Altenberg Lieder* play on the stereo, and warm you up for seeing the production of his opera, *Lulu*, later.

"I do not know this music," Sándor says. "But I love the writing for the voice."

"It's typical for Berg—lyrical but angular."

"You can feel his passion."

"Absolutely. These songs are from 1913 or so, and *Lulu* is much later, from 1935."

"He died that year," he says.

"You're quite the savvy one. Yes, he did die then but completed the first two acts and had a short score for the final act. How do you know so much about music?"

"From early childhood, I studied violin and played in the youth orchestra in Budapest, and later in the university's symphony when I studied in Paris. And I researched this morning."

"Ah. I always wanted to play violin well—I have one, and I get around on it and know how it works, but I really can't play."

"I am sure you play well enough. And *Lulu*? I thought Berg's wife did not want to have the score finished by anyone but Schoenberg," Sándor says.

"Some guy—a Friedrich something—completed the full score after her death and it was premiered in 1979."

"This cycle, *Altenberg Lieder*—beautiful. I love the colors of the orchestra."

"Yes. These songs are dark overall, but this first one of the cycle sparkles."

Your car emerges from the tunnel and you head for Lincoln Center, where you park underneath the complex in the garage. There's plenty of time for dinner before the opera and you and Sándor walk across the street in time for your reservation at P. J. Clarke's.

You're able to order the food when the waiter comes to ask what you want to drink. Sándor requests water with his meal and you hesitate; you want a beer but know you won't be able to leave it at that, so you have water, too. You split an Angry Lobster Cocktail with Sándor and he orders King George's Shepherd's Pie for his entrée and you'll have the Grilled Mahi Mahi Tacos.

By the time you eat and walk across the street to the Met, the ticket line is long, and thick with people. Sándor helps you with your overcoat and stands off to the side, waiting. Your seats are in the orchestra section; you'll be on an aisle, towards the stage in the center.

Sándor's tux emphasizes his broad shoulders and height, and you see women staring up at him as they walk by. He doesn't notice, or pretends not to, and continues to hold your coat, folded neatly over his arm. *He must have had his share of lovers. These women can't stop ogling him.*

You wish you wore something more glamorous. At least

you're formal, black, gauzy pants flaring slightly at the bottom and velvet jacket coming to a V at the front clasp of your brassiere, showing enough skin to make things interesting. Your hair, which you curled in the morning, covers the bulk of your cleavage with its tresses.

You have the tickets and check your coats so you won't have to carry them around all evening. Sándor excuses himself and goes to the men's room, and as you thread your way through the crowd, you see the bar is open.

You can't help yourself, and order a bourbon, which you guzzle. There are two bartenders taking orders so you go to the other end of the bar so the first server won't see you, order another, and gulp that down, too. You're feeling fine. When Sándor returns you give him a sloppy smile.

He frowns.

How does he always know?

8:00 pm

The curtain rises and you're overwhelmed by the use of bold, black brushstrokes projected onto the set. In contrast to blacks and whites, splashes of red strike the eye, setting the audience up for the graphic nature of the action to follow. The opera's introduction begins; the animal trainer stands at his old-fashioned microphone, inviting the audience to visit the array of creatures. Images flash behind him, mutating as they depict animals, humans and the main attraction, Lulu.

Marlis Petersen amazes the audience as she negotiates the challenging vocal lines of Berg's music. She makes a beautiful Lulu—stunning—not merely her voice, but also her body as she cavorts about the stage, straddling her male counterparts and posing in impossible positions up on ladders and tables, bombarding the audience with her sexuality. Both the actors and the images behind them hammer the audience with violent and sensual detail.

During the intermission after Act I, you stand with Sándor in the lobby. You sip your drink, another whiskey, as Sándor raves about the production.

"Yes, it's amazing," you say. "Sexy, eh? And disturbing. Lulu's husbands are almost finished; one more goes down in Act II."

"Lulu is a femme-fatal but has childlike innocence," Sándor says.

"Yep. Both traits doom her—born a victim, she becomes the victim in the end. She is unable to live up to her lovers' expectations of her to be a good wife, and also a sexpot."

"There are parallels in this society. Children are products of their environment. If their lives are shaped by initial suffering and lack of nurturing, what hope do they have as adults?"

Out of the corner of your eye you see someone dart behind a column. When you look directly, you don't see anything unusual, but think of Zoltán. Confused, and flooded with shame, you remember the night in Zoltán's SUV—your betrayal of Coach, and now here with Sándor. *You're as bad as Lulu. You—*

"Alexandra?"

"Oh, sorry. Just spacing out." You let him take your arm, and shake off the frenzy of guilt.

"Let us go in," he says.

You find your seats and the curtain rises for the second act. You watch Sándor, hands gripping the arms of his seat, wide-eyed and captivated. You have to smile. He's like a kid at the circus.

10:37 pm

The second intermission, between Acts Two and Three, begins and you're squirrely. Your pre-opera and first intermission whiskies are long worn off, and you need more. You purchase a double, and walk to the balcony outside, where you overlook the plaza fountain, taking more time with your drink this time. There are a few people there, having a smoke or talking with one another. You lean on the railing and breath in second-hand smoke from someone alongside you, relishing the aroma. Although you stopped smoking just before you and Coach first got together, you still love the smell. You sense someone behind you, and suppose Sándor is there to scold you for drinking again.

"I've been expecting you," a voice says.

Uh-oh.

"This is the fifth performance I've attended, hoping to see you."

"Hello, Sam," you say, as you glance over your shoulder, addled.

"I thought you would be grateful, and happy to see me here," he says, adjusting his wide, dated tie.

"It's just a surprise, that's all. You must know this opera in retrograde inversion by now." You don't want to be unkind, but this is weird, so your sarcasm shows. Sam's thick, wavy hair is a bit greasy, and unruly. You stare at it.

"I was never a big Berg fan. Music by Schoenberg's other disciple is much more elegant, without all the Bergian melodrama."

"Webern. Not melodramatic, true. But this stalking of yours is a bit over-the-top."

Now Sándor does find you, looks from Sam to you and says, "Will you not introduce me?"

"Well, well. This is your much, much older fiancé—this giant man?" Sam says, gawking up at Sándor.

With Sam's needling you think of Coach and lose it. You haven't told Sándor about Coach yet and it pours out.

"My love is dying and you're here pestering me," you say to Sam, "and my father is dead."

"I was sorry to hear about your father. But it looks to me as if you're cozying up to someone new already in spite of your grief," he says, pointing at Sándor.

"This man is a total gentleman, unlike you, you—sawed-off hyena, you."

"There's no need to be rude," Sam says, and retreats into the theater.

You lean on Sándor, sobbing.

11:02 pm

The chimes signal the beginning of the final act, and you're still crying. All Sándor can do is lead you to the coat room, and then head for the garage. Without saying anything, you open your clutch and find your keys, hand them to Sándor and let him open the car door for you. Slumped in your seat, you cry though the tunnel and across the Turnpike, finally settling down a bit when you get on the Parkway.

"I'm sorry," you say, in the midst of your sniffling. "I don't know what to do next. I didn't want to whine at you tonight."

"Alexandra. I understand your anguish. There are some things I cannot see clearly, and while I knew—someday—I would be connected to you, I did not see the illness in Max. All I see is his enduring love for you, and yours for him."

"I already feel lost, and just hope I have him for a little while more, at least."

"That is not for us to know. Try to enjoy the time you do have with him."

"Sándor?"

"Yes?"

"What do you mean when you say we'll be connected?"

"The last time I was in Budapest, about ten years ago, I saw my grandmamma, right before she died. She was one-hundred and two years of age."

"Don't tell me," you say.

"What?"

"Your grandmamma has the gift, too."

"Yes," he says.

"What did she say?"

"She told me my greatest challenge would be the love of my lifetime."

"That could be anyone," you say.

"And she told me this love would bear my name."

"What's that supposed to mean?"

"In Hungarian, Sándor is a name for Alexander."

You're not ready for that, so you frown and look at the window until you doze for the rest of the way home.

Friday, December 4th
2:03 am

"Let us sleep now. I must be home early this morning for György. He will have to have his bath; he enjoys it so."

"A cleanly parrot. Sweet," you murmur.

Sándor makes himself comfortable on your couch and you stumble to the bedroom. The amount you drank was enough to disrupt your body, and your sleep. You study the ceiling, hoping to drift off, and the next thing you know you're sweating and trying to scream. Someone stands over you, and you're frightened.

"Alex, Alex, all is well."

Coach?

You groan and dry-heave over the side of the bed. Large, firm hands cradle your head and guide it back to the pillow. You open your eyes. Zoltán stands leans over, and you shift back in bed, slamming yourself against the headboard.

"Alexandra, it is Sándor. Be still. You need rest. Drink this first," he says.

"Thank you." You sip a bit of water, and put your head down.

Sándor places his cool hand on your forehead, and this

soothes you.

"Try to sleep."

"Don't leave me, please."

Sándor sits on the edge of the bed. Your hair sticks to your cheek and he smooths it back, continuing to caress you until you fall asleep.

Chapter Twelve
Friday, December 4th
7:16 am

You and Sándor drive to the end of his street and sit in the car for a moment, looking beyond the boardwalk towards the rough ocean. It's a dark day, and you're both tired.

"Will you come in for a tea?" he says.

"Thanks, but no. I have to go home and call—" Your throat closes up and you can't get the words out.

Sándor saves you. "I understand."

Still choked up, you say, "I have to thank you for driving last night, and for coming with me. I'm sorry we had to leave early."

"It is okay. I have much to think on, and enjoyed what I saw and heard. I would like to see it again sometime."

"Yes. I have an older, vastly different production of *Lulu* on DVD. Maybe some day—"

"Go home, Alexandra. You need to call. I offer prayer energies for your journey. I am here for you."

You're eager to see Coach so you forego the call and drive directly to his house. His sister Joan answers the door and you panic.

"Oh, Alex. Come in and I'll let him know you're here."

You stand in the entryway and wait, hearing hushed voices from upstairs. Normally, you would go up and find him, but with his sister around, you know your place. You hear Coach's familiar tread on the stairs, and move into the living room.

"Hi," you say.

He embraces you and whispers, "Let's get out of here." He takes your hand and you go to the car.

"How was the opera?"

"Long."

Coach laughs and squeezes your hand. "You must've gotten home late."

"Yeah, well, the drive home was hard."

"You should've let Sándor drive," he says.

You glance at him. There wasn't any sarcasm in his voice, although you wonder what he's thinking.

"Are you mad at me?"

Coach smiles. "No. Someone had to go with you. I didn't like the idea of you going up there yourself."

"Thanks."

"Let's go to your place."

You're both hungry, so you make a light breakfast, fruit over oatmeal, and keep the conversation low-key. After you finish, Coach rises and walks behind your chair. He stoops, kissing the back of your neck. You shiver, bounce up and kiss him on the mouth. You remain in the kitchen for a long while kissing, an odd place for smooches, but that's where the moment is.

"You haven't had your shower today," he says.

"Ugh, do I smell?"

He laughs and buries his face in your hair. "Not at all. But it's a good excuse to shower with you. I didn't take one, either."

He removes your shirt and pants in the midst of kisses—on your tummy, your thighs and up to your neck again. You can't help but giggle, and pull his sweater over his shoulders, fumbling with the zipper of his jeans. You leave your clothes in the kitchen and kiss your way to the bathroom; then you draw a bath.

Your need to relax with Coach eclipses your need for cleanliness, and you want to feel him against you, rather than having to stand in the shower. The tub sits above the floor, but plenty big enough for two. The warm water, bubbly and soft, caresses your bodies and after a while, Coach soaps your legs, which straddle him and they give his body a squeeze.

"Hey, Lovey," you say, "let's shower off and retire to the bedroom."

2:51 pm

"Joanie's probably wondering if you kidnapped me."

"I did," you say and stretch, turning over to face him. "I want to stay here in bed with you into the night and then all day tomorrow."

"I should get back. Let's do this again soon." Coach kisses your forehead and goes to the kitchen. You watch him walk, admiring his still-muscled body, especially his sweet bottom. You whistle at him as he walks out the door.

When you get to Coach's house, you sit in the car for a while, holding hands. His hair is askew from sleeping; you reach over and ruffle it. "I love you so much." Tears roll down your cheeks.

"I know you do, Sweetheart. I'll see you soon." He pecks you on the cheek and as you wipe your eyes with your shirt, he says, "I love you with all my heart." He turns your chin towards him and kisses you. You don't want him to stop. Unable to speak, you stretch your arm over and give his behind a pinch as he gets out of the car. Your mouth trembles and a smile is not going to happen. All you can do is watch him walk away.

Sunday, December 6th
7:46 pm

Joan decides to stay a few more days, and you haven't seen much of Coach. You feel lucky you had Friday together, but hope for more. You've been sleeping, or trying to, all weekend except for going to church, which was long. Although it's Advent and the service music is lovely, you feel like staying home unless you're with him. Alcohol is a close second in your mind, but you haven't indulged. It breaks your heart—not sharing your nights with Coach—and you just want his sister to go home.

You could've been the one to come first, but, no. Why didn't you marry him long ago? Because. You're selfish and full of yourself.

The kitchen cabinet beckons.

You return to the bedroom with a tumbler. Jefferson lounges on the bed and you can't bring yourself to kick him off, so you go to the desk, open Facetime and call Dennis. He doesn't answer but calls you back after five minutes.

"Hi, Alex. How're you doing?"

"Okay. As well as I can, considering. How about you?"

"Cold. Seems like it rains or snows every day up here."

"That's icky," you say. "Do you have plans for Christmas?"

"I think I'm going to Florida to see my mom," he says.

"The cabin must feel empty, so I'm glad you won't be stuck there over the holidays."

"Yes, me, too. How's Max?"

"Tired. I haven't seen that much of him because his sister is staying at his house. She's leaving Wednesday or Thursday for a couple of days but she'll be back."

"How's that going?"

You take a big gulp of whiskey, and it goes down the wrong way. "Ugh. Sorry, Dennis." After you clear your throat and cough, you recover. "She's nice enough with me. I think the age difference bothers her more than anything."

"I had a similar situation with your Dad. It was only a fifteen-year gap, but still raised some eyebrows among his older cronies. And then, many weren't thrilled with our openly gay relationship."

"Even I totally understood your relationship. You were great for Dad. You were lucky to have one another." You pause and sigh.

"It's hard to believe Max is sick. He always looks so healthy; even when he came up for the memorial service he looked great."

"It's insidious, this cancer thing. In Max's case, it's advanced and inoperable."

"I'm so sorry. Hang on as well as you can, and try to make the most of the time you have. I know it's hard."

You finish your drink, swilling it back quickly so you won't cry. "Well, that's life, I guess. I hope you rest well, Dennis."

"You, too."

Monday, December 7th
9:02 am

The phone rings and you look at the clock, stunned because you've slept so late. As usual, you can't find the damn thing. The sound comes from your chair, which is piled with dirty clothes. You rummage around and find it behind the cushion. It's Coach, and he's gone by the time you answer. *Shit.* When you call back, he picks up after two rings.

"Morning," he says.

"Hey. What's up?"

"Joanie's at the grocery store. She stocks the fridge with more than I can ever use."

"She's just being a good sister," you say.

"I know. But I'm tired of all the mollycoddling."

"I'll coddle your molly for you."

"That sounds nice. Can I come over?" he says.

"Sure. Let me clean myself up and let Jefferson out. He's staring at me."

Coach arrives and suggests that you take a walk with the beagle. You call Jefferson and he patters out of the kitchen, then you fasten his harness and get his sweater out of a drawer. He wags his tail and lets you slip the sweater over his head then you attach the leash to the harness. It's chilly although the sun is bright. Jefferson pulls you down the road, stopping at almost every tree.

"It's amazing he tolerates those sweaters you make him wear."

"He knows if I get his sweater out he's going for a walk. That's why."

After a while, Coach stops, placing his hand to his forehead. "Hmmm," he says.

"Are you okay?"

"Sure. I'm just tired."

"We should go back," you say, pulling the beagle away from a fire hydrant. Coach moves slower going home. Concerned, you take his hand, and don't let Jefferson sniff every blade of grass along the way. When you reach the condo, you get the beagle settled and bring Coach a glass of water. He falls asleep in the recliner and you sit on the floor next to it, resting your head against his thigh. It takes you a long time to fall asleep, and just after you do Coach's phone rings. He doesn't hear it so you tap his knee and wake him. By the time he rouses himself, the phone isn't ringing, but he checks to see who it is.

"Joanie must be home. I should really go. She's probably leaving Wednesday morning, and who knows what's up after that."

"Uh-huh. Can you come back later?"

"After she goes home I'll spend every night from then on with you. Okay?"

"Promise?"

"Yup." He puts his arm around your shoulders as you walk him to the door. "I love you, Alex."

"I love you, too. Heaps."

You watch him from the window. He waves as he backs out of the space and then drives away.

Tuesday, December 8th
6:13 pm

You're out of sorts, pacing back and forth. You sat at your computer for a long while working on your requiem mass and your butt's sore. The walking helps your body but your mind races. You haven't heard from Coach since last night, and you're angry with his sister for keeping him away from you. At least she's leaving tomorrow. You shouldn't call him but you have to. A woman's voice answers.

"Alex, hang on," she says.

"Joan?"

You hear muffled voices and clatter. Her hand must be muting the phone. After about two minutes, she's back. "Alex. I don't know what to say. I was going to call you and with all of the family calls—"

"What's wrong?" you say, your voice tight. You had to ask her, but you know, oh, you know what's wrong. Before Joan can answer you say, "It's Max."

She's silent.

"What happened?"

"I'm sorry, Alex. Max had a brain embolism this afternoon. The doctor said he wouldn't have felt anything, but he's gone."

You don't hear any more and drop the phone.

Chapter Thirteen
Tuesday, December 15th
9:45 am

Coach's wake and mass are today and you consider not going. You've been in bed all week and didn't go to church. You and Coach have mutual acquaintances, and you know some of his friends. Other than that, you're on your own. You can't ask Sándor to come with you to this one.

Mass takes place at the same Catholic church where you made your mangled confession last month. At least the priest won't recognize you without your clown clothes. As usual, you struggle to find something appropriate to wear. Black is not the problem; you have oodles of dark-colored clothing. Most of it is formal, the sort of flashy thing you can perform in rather than mourn someone in. You choose a black suit, lay it out on the bed and start the shower. You'll have to shave your legs because you won't wear pantyhose—they give you fits—and the shower takes longer than you want. If you hurry you can make mass on time.

By the time you arrive, people are lined up outside the door of the church. There'll be standing room only, like a sold-out performance. You manage to squeeze into the last pew next to a few awkward looking teenage boys, some with a bit of mustache already, some wearing glasses, all dressed nicely in shirts and ties, kids from Coach's high school.

You watch people file slowly down the middle aisle, and notice a long line of boys wearing green and white jerseys—Coach's freshman football team. Some of them are bigger than others, and you see László among them, tall and lanky. You should line up with everyone and greet the family, but can't bear to, so you remain where you are.

The service begins. Coach's family sits in the front row—his sister and her husband, his two nieces and a nephew with their teenage children. Coach's nieces read the scripture verses, and when it's time for people to speak a few words celebrating Coach, his sister talks briefly. She focuses on the joy he brought others with his easy laugh and positive attitude, his strength of character and purpose, and his fierce loyalty to family and friends. His nephew tells some funny stories, and then two of his fellow faculty members from school speak, the second being the athletic director.

"I extend my deepest sympathies to Max's family, and his partner, Alex," he says, and talks about Coach's service to the school, both as an English teacher and football coach.

Finally, you're a part of things.

On the way home, you go out of your way to a liquor store that will actually sell to you, and purchase two cases of beer. After you load the car you go back into the store and buy a carton of Marlboros. You make yourself not smoke until you can bundle up and sit in your favorite chair on the deck. Jefferson will need to go out anyway.

You sit with a beer in one hand and a cigarette in the other, fat and squishy in your bright purple puffer coat. Jefferson approaches to see if you have a biscuit in your pocket, but backs away quickly, sneezing from the smoke. This makes you feel bad. After your fifth beer, a heavy-handed melancholia plagues you. Sweaty and chilled, you go inside, take the phone out of your pocket and stare at it. You could call Dennis, but he's busy in the middle of the week. That only leaves Sándor, and you haven't been talking to him much. He's probably swamped with clients, anyway. You'll wait until early evening to call, and sleep off your five beers instead.

Saturday, December 19th
6:31 pm

You never do call anyone, not even Sándor. You've been in a cycle of drinking and sleeping for days, and while beer usually makes you hungry, you haven't been eating much. You're bloated nevertheless, and the only thing you've done is lie in bed with your beer, watching the Weather Channel. When you feel like having a cigarette, only then do you let the beagle out.

You finally call Sándor and he answers, but you're crying again and can't speak.

"Alexandra, I know. Peace."

You sob harder and crack open the first beer of your third round of the day. "I can't believe he's not here."

"I cannot speak with you while you are—doing that."

"Doing what?"

"Alexandra. We cannot think clearly when you are drinking."

You remain silent as he continues.

"I am profoundly saddened by your loss, and my heart aches on your behalf. But you must learn to face this without dulling your senses."

"Oh, what's the difference," you bark, and then add, "If we can't talk on the phone, can you come over?"

"No. I am sorry. That would not be good. Try and sleep."

"I've been sleeping."

"I will send you healing prayers."

Thursday, December 24th
8:32 pm

You force yourself to take a shower and dress, after about ten days of wallowing in it. Father Marcus and Maestro Healey understand why you missed so much church, but want you there this evening for midnight mass. The beagle follows you to the door, grinning up at you.

Thank God for dogs.

You stoop and scratch him behind his ears, and as an afterthought, go back to the kitchen and get him a treat. He gobbles it up without chewing most of it and coughs, ready for the next one. A hint of a smile plays at your lips, but recedes as you think of Coach again.

Choir rehearsal is easy tonight. For Christmas Eve, you usually sing familiar, although challenging things. As you practice the "Halleluiah Chorus" from Handel's *Messiah*, you focus on the alto part and your mind doesn't race.

Before rehearsal many members of the choir came up to you and offered sympathy for your loss. Somehow this makes you feel better and less isolated from the world. You don't have to wear choir robes this evening, and everyone is decked out in bright reds and greens, sparkly silvers and golds, their Christmas best. You wear black.

The church is decorated with holly and garlands at the stained-glass windows, and candles; the Advent Wreath, all candles lit for Christmas, hangs from the ceiling. And poinsettias. There are poinsettias everywhere, bright red ones. You consider leaving after you sing the anthem, but make yourself stay until the very end of the service, after the organ postlude. By then it's after midnight, and you're ready to go home.

You spent the last two Christmases with Coach, the first in Bermuda, and the second you woke up with him in your bed Christmas morning. This year, you don't feel any of the normal Christmas anticipation or excitement. Your emotions are flattened by so much loss. Earlier today, a glimmer of gratitude, faint but present, opened your mind to accepting Sándor's invitation to spend Christmas day with him and László.

Before you go in the condo, you pause. The night is clear, and you look up at the sky and see the moon, which must be full. You unlock the door and Jefferson greets you. After you let him outside you put some Christmas music on. You have a few presents to wrap.

Friday, December 25th

9:47 am

You text Sándor after you're parked in his driveway. The garage door opens and you close the door and climb the stairs, lugging two shopping bags. You walk through the pool area, house and into the kitchen; when you see Sándor you smile in spite of yourself. He wears a red sweater and jeans, partially covered by a long, embroidered apron, bright green with candy canes and red Santa Clauses on it. He returns your smile, embraces you, and kisses you on one cheek, then the other.

"Merry Christmas, Alexandra."

"Merry, merry to you, too. Where's László?"

"He is just stirring now. We were awake until late. You were short on sleep as well, with midnight mass?"

"I slept for a good six hours, thanks. That's enough."

"Yippee! Home run, home run."

You turn toward the voice and see György sits on a branch of the large tree in his cage, hopping from one foot to the other.

"Home run?" you say.

To your surprise, Sándor blushes. "Ah. I do not care for television so much, but during baseball season, I have to watch. I am quite taken with the game, and often," he pauses, smiling sheepishly, "shout at the television."

"C'mon, c'mon, home run!" György croaks.

You laugh. "It's not baseball season, György. Merry Christmas, anyway."

The parrot flies from where he's sitting to a closer perch. "Yippee!"

"The fire smells great. But isn't this warm weather weird?" you say.

"Yes. And did you notice the full moon?"

"I did see it. Thought it must be full."

A Christmas tree stands in the corner opposite György's cage, decorated with blue and white lights, and shiny blue and silver ornaments. You grab the shopping bag with the presents. The ceiling is high and the tree almost touches it.

"How did you ever get this tree in here?" you say over your shoulder.

"The movers helped. They are clients of mine. Of course, I needed the ladder to reach the higher parts as I decorated," Sándor says.

"You did a beautiful job."

László enters the kitchen, rubbing his eyes as he yawns.

"Did you sleep enough?" Sándor says, embracing his nephew.

"I think so," László says, and sits on a stool. "I'm still not awake."

"I have a tea for us," he says, just as the kettle begins to whistle.

You lay the presents under the tree and then serve the tea for Sándor, who busies himself with the oven. The aroma of bacon fills the kitchen, along with smells of cinnamon and wood smoke.

"May I help with anything?"

Sándor closes the oven and stands to his full height. "You can take the bowl of fruit out of the refrigerator, and László can finish setting the table," he says and turns to his nephew. "You will feel more awake if you move around." He ruffles László's hair and attends to the stove. László rousts himself from the stool and moves to a cupboard, where linens and silverware are stored.

As usual, you're struck by how imposing Sándor is, and also by his warmth and kindness. He makes his house livable, human and homey; you feel comfortable and welcome here.

"Would you like sausage also or is bacon alone good?" he says.

"I'm happy with bacon, thanks. How about you, László?" you say.

He considers as he folds a napkin. "Bacon works for me."

Sándor finishes with the eggs and covers them with a lid. The potatoes are done, fried with onions and peppers. The tray of pastries you brought and a bowl of mixed nuts sit on the table, along with a carafe of fresh coffee. Sándor drains the bacon and puts that on the table with the rest of the feast.

You sit, and Sándor, at the head of the table, extends his hands to you and László, on either side of him. As you grasp hands, he says a blessing, and then you dig into the food.

"It's such a warm day. Do we have plans for later?" you say.

Sándor looks towards the window and smiles. "I have an idea."

"I'd like to take a nap," László says.

"There is time for sleeping later this afternoon. I have a surprise for us after we break our fast."

"I love surprises," you say. "Will one of you please pass the bread?"

Sándor hands you the basket, and you choose a croissant. He hasn't mentioned anything about your troubles or recent behavior, but you often catch him stealing a glance at you. Your eyes meet and he smiles again. "You look good today. How are you feeling?"

You sigh. "I'm grateful to be here, for the wonderful company and food." That's all you can say because you'll start crying. You sit up straighter and shake your tears off, making your face brighter. "I want to hear more about this surprise."

"If the wind is enough there is something I would like to try."

"Wind?" you say.

"When I stopped in Jakarta on my way to Bali a few years ago, I purchased a souvenir, and it is still in its package."

"Sounds intriguing."

László finishes chewing his bacon and laughs. "My uncle likes to keep us in suspense."

"I will go and get it," Sándor says, as he clears his plate and takes it to the sink.

After he's gone, László looks at you but doesn't speak. You're uncomfortable, so you say, "Is something wrong?"

"No. I just, well, I'm sorry about Coach Max. He was great."

You manage a smile. "Thank you. I saw you at mass with the team. That was a nice tribute."

"We'll miss him."

"Yeah, me too."

Sándor returns with something large and colorful wrapped in clear plastic.

"What's that?" László says.

"A kite?" you ask.

"That is exactly right. The bird kites of Indonesia are made from hand-painted silk," Sándor says as he unwraps and discards the plastic.

László goes to the deck and checks to see if it's windy enough. Sándor unfolds the kite.

"Ooh, that's beautiful. I love the purples, pinks and blues—so colorful."

"Yes." He puts the kite on a chair and turns to you. "How are you feeling?"

"I'm grateful to have a place to go on Christmas Day. And it's more than that. Thank you for sharing your home and László with me. He's a fun kid, and you are—" You stop and you feel your face turn red, leaving it at that. Sándor must know what you're thinking and gives you a brief hug.

"There's a little breeze—probably enough," László says, returning. He picks up the kite and examines it. "It's a little girly, isn't it?" László doesn't exhibit much enthusiasm but you can tell he likes the idea.

You walk up the ramp of the boardwalk. Although the tide is low, there isn't much of a beach because of erosion from storms. There's enough to move around some and fly the kite.

László tries first; after a few attempts, the wind catches the kite and it takes a nosedive in the sand. "Here, you do it," he says to his uncle.

Sándor holds the kite with his arms stretched above him until the wind catches it. Finally, it takes off. After a while he gives you the handle and says, "Let more string out and the wind will take it." You run with the kite; the wind carries it farther down the beach.

"Don't fly away," László yells over the roar of the ocean.

You laugh, releasing some of your tension. Sándor stands with his hands on his hips, then waves and jogs towards you. "You are soaring, Alexandra!"

4:51 pm

You're all tired from the sun and kite flying. It's time for you to leave. You don't want to. The prospect of going back to your beer and solitude isn't thrilling. But you have to care for the beagle.

"I had a great time. Please thank László again for me."

"Next time, you can bring the dog and stay longer. György will not mind," Sándor says.

"Thanks, we'll try it."

Sándor kisses you on both cheeks and gives you a hug. "Remember, Alexandra, you have choices in this life. You can allow everything to push you down or you can climb from the mire and soar. Be good to yourself."

Chapter Fourteen
Wednesday, December 30th
1:37 pm

For the next few weeks, there isn't much going on except church. You sober up enough to get there and back on Sunday, but other than that you're drunk. The New Year approaches, and you won't go out—nothing to celebrate. When you wake up the day after Christmas you feel better after two days sober, but start in again, hitting it hard. You're just awake after sleeping off your first round of the day and on impulse call Sándor.

"Hello, my friend. How are you feeling?" he says.

"Not so good. But I have an idea."

"What is it?"

"You probably know I haven't been very good about taking care of myself. If you come over for New Year's Eve, I'll be good, and that'll motivate me to clean up and—"

"I am sorry, but I am booked into tomorrow evening. My clients are in a rush to plan for the next year, and have been calling to see me."

You're quiet for a moment as tears pool in your eyes; you swallow the lump out of your throat, and say, "That's okay. I understand. Well, Happy New Year, almost." You hang up before he has a chance to answer.

It hits you bad—your dirty, cluttered condo doesn't help. You've been tossing your beer cans across your bedroom, aiming for the wicker clothes basket in the corner. Most of the time you miss. You'd stop battering yourself with drink for a while if only Sándor would come to visit. Now there's nothing but hoo-hah.

Sunday, January 3rd 2016
10:42 am

After everyone greets one another during the Peace, Father Marcus asks for announcements, and various people say what they have to say, including a woman who begs everyone to take a poinsettia home. The flowers are all over the church, and even if every member of the congregation took one, there would be more. Maybe the mess in your condo wouldn't seem so bad if you littered every room with poinsettias.

The choir lines up in front for the anthem. Today you're singing another Handel piece, *Zadok the Priest*, and you think you'll name your next beagle after good ol' Zadok. You space out when you're well into the Handel, and accidentally jump up to the soprano part, obvious because your singing voice is so loud and now the altos struggle in your absence. Maestro Healey darts a glare in your direction as he conducts from the piano.

Oops.

He knows you fucked up. You wipe the smirk off your puss and continue singing. Now you just want to get out of here. You wait for Healey to finish the organ postlude before you leave—nice of you, given you're sweating like a pig and have a monstrous headache.

You ditch the choir robe and make for the exit. People carry poinsettias to their cars. Many flowers are left throughout the church after everyone leaves. You haul three plants to the car, open the trunk and put them in. Then you go and get three more.

Thursday, January 7th
3:31 am

The refrigerator is empty. You've already had pizza delivered twice this week, and they're closed at this time of night anyway. Tired and wired, you can't sleep or do anything productive—not that you want to work. You should have some coffee but continue with beer instead, pounding them down until you pass out.

When you finally open your eyes the smell hits you, and you feel Jefferson stretched out on the bed by your side, licking your hand as he whines. You sit up and see a fresh pile on the floor in a patch of sunlight. "Poor little thing," you say, and cringe as you both avoid the mess. Jeffrey follows you to the slider, happy when you let him out. You clean up the poop, go to the kitchen and fill his food bowl. His water bowl is empty and you feel even worse.

Jeffrey soon barks at the door; you let him in and he goes straight to his water. "I'm so sorry, Peep." He looks over his shoulder at you, tail wagging, and then attacks his food. *Enough is enough.* Once the beagle is settled on the recliner in the living room, you take a shower and recycle all the empties.

7:02 pm

To your surprise, someone knocks at the door. You're not a fan of the pop-in, so you're glad you tidied up. At first you hesitate. The knocking continues, and you move to the door, catching your reflection in the mirror along the way. You're clean and your hair's shiny, but your eyes are sunken and dark underneath.

Oh, well.

You peek out the window and see Sándor holding a large, lidded pot of something; relief washes over you—not because you expected someone else, but because you won't be alone for once.

"Hello, Alexandra."

"Please come in."

"I thought you would like to have a soup. I am not able to stay long."

Your heart sinks, then you rally. "Thank you. I haven't had the chance to get to the store." That's a lie. You've been so drunk you haven't been fit for driving anywhere. Sándor takes the pot to the kitchen, puts it on the stove and lights the burner.

"Can you stay long enough to have some with me?" you say as he sits at the kitchen table.

You think he's considering but notice he's staring at something. You follow to where he's looking and see the six poinsettias lined up on the hearth. "What?" you say.

"I apologize. I thought I saw—"

"Saw something. Like a ghost?" You worry about ghosts sometimes—ghosts and demons.

"No," he says and pauses. "I had a vision."

"I wondered if you're able to see ahead deliberately and with how much detail."

"They come and go, and happen in fragments. Often, I do not know what they mean until much later. And at times, I sense things."

He rubs his forehead.

"Are you okay?" you say.

"I am tired now. The visions exhaust me, even though they are usually brief."

"Would soup help?"

"No, thank you. I think I will go now." He stands slowly as if dizzy, and you don't push him to stay. You walk with him to the door and he turns towards you. "Please, take care."

"Oh, don't worry about me. I'll be fine," you say, trying to laugh.

"I am serious. I do care much for you."

"Really?"

"Of course. Do not be a silly."

"Same here." Your face reddens and you look away.

"Goodbye, My Dear."

"See you around."

Sunday, January 10th
1:01 pm

As usual, church is long. When you get home, you take care of the beagle and sleep. You've been trying not to drink since Sándor stopped by, and can't bear it anymore. Although you know where you are, you feel lost in the gaping hole where your favorite two people made their home in your heart. It's Sunday, the day to FaceTime with your father. You're grateful Dennis likes you, and you'll speak with him later. But it's not the same.

And Coach.

His extraordinary patience with your myriad of foibles astounds you still—like your reluctance to use public restroom facilities. When on the golf course with Coach he'd step into the woods when he had to go. You wouldn't do that so you whined about having to go for the remainder of the nine holes, and wouldn't use the bathroom in the clubhouse either, and continued to whinge in the car until you got home.

He laughed off your grousing, except when he had the sports station on the radio set too loud in the car. The chatter of the broadcasters annoyed you. Then you couldn't help yourself and turned the radio off. Coach would flip out and say when you drive you can blast whatever artsy-fartsy thing you want.

You crack open a beer and go to the stereo system. Olivier Messiaen's *Turangalila-Symphonie* is in the CD player and usually makes you giggle, delighted by its flamboyancy, gestures of remarkable color and joyful abandon.

Today you'll cut to the chase and go for the dark heavyweight, Gustav Mahler. His Sixth Symphony, your favorite, is subtitled *Tragic*. The sounds of low string instruments grinding out the four rump, rump, rump rumps of the opening measure punch you in the gut, and you immerse yourself in the rest of the movement.

As you listen you slow down with your beer, and eventually stand to conduct the final movement of the symphony in front of the stereo system. Lenny sure gets his tempos right—you wouldn't do anything different. In the fourth, final movement, you love the presence of the *Almglocken*—tuned cowbells—during the sections of murky calm, you love the heroic melodic lines in the brass as the musical drama heightens. Most of all you love the Mahler Hammer, played at the climaxes, and in the final measures of the piece.

By now you're sweating and exhausted. You stand still and think of the time you saw Klaus Tennstedt conduct this piece with Philly, and people applauded before the final pizzicato. He looked sad when he turned around to face the audience, and was gracious in spite of. As much as you prefer your Bernstein Mahler recordings, you treasure the concert time with Maestro Tennstedt, grateful you saw him conduct before he died.

After the Mahler finishes, you're left with nothing but silence, and the sound of your ragged breathing. The beagle follows you out the door when you go for a smoke, and you sit in your deteriorating beach chair, sobbing as you take one last puff. You put the cigarette in the ashcan; Jefferson approaches when the smoke clears, and sits in front of you. You can't stop crying and lean with your face in your hands, rocking forward and back. Jefferson paws at your knee; your tears spent, you reach out and stroke the soft fur on his ears.

Chapter Fifteen
Wednesday, January 20th
8:32 pm

You've been drunk for days, for so long you're losing track. The trashed condo smells rancid and it's not good for you or Jefferson. At least you haven't smoked inside. You consider hiring a cleaning service, but need to do some sort of penance. You start by getting rid of the clutter of empty beer cans, which you've left all over the place, from the mantle of the fireplace to the counter around the bathroom sink. The stench hits you again and again, the odor of a sticky floor in a seedy tavern.

You don't know whether to scrub the floors or vacuum, so you use a broom to sweep up crumbs and bits of trash instead, and then get the vacuum and go over the carpets. You fill a bucket with water and cleaning detergent, and with a cloth you work on your hands and knees, getting the grunge off the tile floors, wiping the cabinets off where you slopped things on them, and you clean the windows. Jefferson watches from his seat on the couch. You often pause to pet him.

Into the night you clean, without drinking to accompany you, without tears, without angst. For the first time in many days, you feel something approaching peace. The last thing you do before you shower is water the poinsettias. "Here you go, Boys." You make sure the earth in the pots is moist enough; you heard poinsettias don't like much water. After you let Jefferson out again you take a shower and put fresh sheets on the bed. When you're settled you snuggle close to Jefferson, your arm around him as he purrs you to sleep.

Thursday, January 21st
2:23 pm

You only rise to care for the beagle. The sense of peace you feel throughout the night carries into the day, and you're able to rest with the condo smelling fresh, the clutter gone and your body clean. You might even go to church Sunday if the weather is clear by then. The forecast predicts snow for the weekend and you want to get your grocery shopping done before that happens.

For a while you enjoy the day. You make it to the store and the kitchen is stocked with wholesome foods. You haven't relaxed in a long time although you've slept off the alcohol. Now you try not to think ahead. You spend the rest of the afternoon going through papers and paying bills. When you finish your tasks, there's nothing left to do. Sándor might call or stop by; you know he's sick of your drunken shenanigans and the way you've handled your grief. As your mind clears it hits you—you're alone.

Friday, January 22nd
4:52 pm

You tried to compose last night and again this morning. The music wouldn't flow and you spent more time staring at the computer screen than entering notes. You slept as much as you could over the last two days and now you can't rest. You pace the floor in the bedroom and finally go to the living room to see what Jefferson is doing. He's by the slider watching the birds and squirrels at the feeder.

There are no cardinals this afternoon; it's the time of day they usually appear—dusk—and you're saddened by their absence. You let Jefferson out and get a glass of water, drinking what you want and give the rest to one of the poinsettias, although they probably don't need more. They've thrived in spite of the stagnant atmosphere in the condo, filling out just in two weeks, bushy with red leaves and healthy-looking stems.

Since you were a child, you've given names to things, from cars and computers to plants and even favorite keepsakes. You once had a car named Wally. Now you call the poinsettias Fred, one living organism there to entertain and keep you company.

Jefferson prances through the slider and you give him his evening food and refill his water bowl. He doesn't eat at first, holding out for something better; you don't want any dinner and disappoint him. He gobbles his food, looking at you to make sure you know how much he loves it.

You plop on the recliner in the living room, Coach's chair, and your stomach sinks. Then you rise and pace, moving from one end of the room to the other until you wear yourself down. By now it's dark and you sit again, not bothering to turn on any lights. You spin the recliner until you face the fireplace and see Fred, still in his Christmas glory. The holidays are over; your father and Coach are dead.

It's still early and the kennel might be open and have room for Jefferson. You call and they do have space. You bundle him up, gather his things and take him to the car. You're quiet on the way and he must wonder where you're going. When you get there, you sit in the car for a few minutes, stroking his fur and talking to him, and then you take his things in and pay the guy who runs the kennel. You tell him you're not sure how long you need Jefferson to stay, but will call when you figure that out. When you return to the car you open the door and hold the beagle in your arms, hugging him close as you carry him inside. "I love you, Sweet." You leave him with a final hug.

After you get home, you put pajamas on and approach the hearth, your steps slow and deliberate. You bend over Fred and pluck the leaves one by one, crushing them in your free hand. When there are too many to hold you get a bowl from the mantle, one decorated with wintery designs, and put the leaves in it until it's piled high and Fred is skeletal.

The water boils; you immerse the leaves in it, and let it steep. You have no idea how many leaves it takes, but assume the amount you're using will do the trick.

Saturday, January 23rd
6:44 am

The snow is already deep in drifts formed by the wind on the deck. The hemlock trees droop under its weight. You won't be going out today. The poinsettia tea steeped all night. You strain it into a mug, heat it up in the microwave and leave the kitchen, passing by your mother on your way to the bedroom. Maybe she'll forgive you.

Bottoms up.

The tea tastes bitter. You drink it, heat another and while you're waiting you go to the closet in the front hall and take Coach's state championship football jacket out—the one piece of him you have left. You hold it to your face to see if it still smells like him. The scent is vague—a combination of Old Spice, Head and Shoulders and Brylcreem.

He'd sing the Brylcreem theme song for you—out of tune but hilarious with his goofy smile—and how you'd laugh. *A little dab'll do ya.* You get your mug and sit in front of the fireplace. The tea isn't quite as hot this time and you gulp it down. After your third, it's almost gone.

2:59 pm

You wake with a start, realizing you're sleeping the afternoon away. With Coach's jacket draped over you, you're hot and stiff from sitting in an awkward position on the recliner so you stand and stretch. Then you remember. Other than feeling nauseous you're fine, although disappointed. You wonder about the toxicity of poinsettias—you've always heard they're poisonous—or is that only for cats?

It's still snowing and the condo is colder than it was earlier, which feels good, and you leave the thermostat set where it is. If you had any alcohol left you'd drink it, but you cleaned all that up three days ago. Agitated, you rifle through the medicine cabinet. There isn't much in there except for toiletries and an old, crusty bottle of cough medicine.

In the top right corner, there's a bottle of something you can't reach. On tiptoe, you knock it onto the counter below and it spills. The label is faded although you see it's a bottle of over-the-counter sleeping tablets. You wipe off the ones that landed in the sink. There's half a bottle. Without thinking you wash them down with the ancient cough syrup and water. The wind howls. Shivering, you crawl in bed; soon you sleep.

8:37 pm

You're strapped down. A grating, high-pitched buzzing assaults your ears. A clown bends over you with a large drill he's about to put in your mouth. At first, it's the sound that frightens you more than anything. He won't be able to fix that one small cavity without destroying the rest of your teeth. You cringe and squirm in your seat with your mouth shut tight and hope he'll take his drill and go away.

The sense of fear is overwhelming and you're mildly aware your pants are wet. Anyone would lose the contents of their bladder when faced with a drill-wielding clown-dentist. Then you feel yourself being lifted. Sándor, no, Zoltán, carries you away from the madman with the drill. *Out of the frying pan and into—*

"Alexandra," he says, patting your cheek.

"It's okay," you say.

"Alex, where is the dog?"

This is baffling at first and as you reach into your mind it occurs to you someone stole Jefferson. You panic, snapping you into consciousness for a moment.

"Away. Ken," you slur.

"Who is this Ken?"

“K-E-N-N-E.” You always spell the word out when Jeffrey’s around so he won’t think he’s going there.

“Is Jefferson at the kennel?”

“Yah,” you say.

“Alexandra, how many pills did you take?” one of them says.

“Sleepy.”

“You have to go to the hospital.”

“Um-no.”

Sándor and Zoltán argue, their voices distant as you settle into sleep.

Chapter Sixteen
Sunday, January 24th
1:03 am

They make you drink charcoal, the thick, black liquid that absorbs toxins, and monitor your vital signs as you lay in bed in the ER. You're weak and dizzy after they take what could only be two gallons of your blood for testing. Why so much? You doze.

Your head nods and jerks up; you notice Sándor asleep, his legs stretched out so far you can't see his feet because they're under the bed. That chair is way too small for him. He should have a bigger one. Maybe you'll press the call button so someone can find a better chair for Sándor.

After you sleep again you have to relieve yourself, so you do press the button. A short while later a nurse comes in and helps you up, removing the monitors from your finger and arm. Sándor stirs and sits up, rubbing his eyes. You wave as you pass him on the way to the bathroom.

For the next few hours you sleep and go to the toilet over and over, the charcoal ripping through your system. You don't know what time it is, night or day, and wonder how long you've been here. Sándor isn't in the chair and you hope he returns. You're exhausted, although don't want to sleep, peering out the curtained doorway to the activity. Nurses bustle around or sit behind the desk across from you, and people push carts past your cubby, with dirty laundry or trays of food. Your stomach growls and churns, empty by now; you want breakfast.

Sándor pulls the curtain aside and enters with a large coffee, sits and leans forward with a frown.

You frown back.

"How are you feeling?" he says.

"Like a truck hit me."

"That is understandable."

"I think your ordeal was worse than mine."

"Alexandra. Someone will come soon and ask questions, evaluate your situation. They might send you away."

"I've got to pick Jeffrey up. He hates the kennel."

"You need help—beyond what I am able to do."

You pause as tears form in your eyes and roll down your cheeks. "How did you know?"

Sándor considers. "In the vision, I saw the poinsettia plants without leaves, standing like corpses. I did not know at the time what it meant. Yesterday I sensed your distress."

"Why was Zoltán with you?"

"I could not open the door. Zoltán came with the power tools for opening. We called the 9-1-1 number and they came and brought you here. It is good there were not many sleeping pills."

"I'm so sorry," you say.

"Please. Try not to worry. You will get the care you need. Would it help you to know Jefferson is with me? I will get him and he is welcome to stay with myself and László."

"Yes, yes, please. He would like that."

"I will go to the car and bring your purse. We found your phone before we brought you here, and you will be able to make the calls you need."

"Thanks."

4:40 pm

You don't like her—not only because hair frames her tiny, heart-shaped face like a mauve-colored helmet, impeccable and dainty, but also her tone of voice is pleasant—too pleasant. Her open-collared blouse with light green and white stripes complements pants of the same green color. Her fingernails, coated with light pink polish, manicured. She looks more like a docent of an art museum than someone interviewing a crazy person.

"Have you had thoughts of harming yourself at any other point in your life?"

You reach into your mind, think of your teenage years, and shake off a chill. "After my mother died I had a hard time. I don't remember much. My guidance counselor recommended therapy for me. I—" You stop and show her the scars.

"Did you have a suicide attempt?"

"No. The cutting worked well enough."

She's quiet and takes more notes. The sound of the pen on paper grinds against your nerves.

"When did you begin to have suicidal thoughts?" she continues.

You take a moment. "Mid-December, I guess."

"Did any event precipitate the suicidal thoughts?"

"After my father died I learned the man I wanted to marry was sick—very sick," you say.

"How often did you think about suicide?"

You sigh. "It started shortly after Max—his name was Max—died, too, and I felt so low it all didn't seem worth it."

"What makes you feel better?"

Not much.

Then you think of alcohol but your honesty is selective. "My dog."

"What makes you feel worse?"

"All the things that should make me feel better make things worse, except my dog."

"Did you have a plan to end your life?"

"Yes. It failed. Then I tried something else and that worked for a while." You tell her what happened—the house cleaning, taking Jefferson to the kennel, the poinsettias, the sleeping pills and how Sándor found you and called 9-1-1. She scribbles as you speak. You sit up straighter, but can't tell what she's writing. When she looks at you again, your gut's in a total uproar.

"Do you have a history of substance abuse?"

"No," you say without missing a beat, and hope your face didn't redden.

She looks at her notes again.

Phew.

"I recommend you go to a hospital for care and assessment," she says.

"For how long?" you croak.

"A doctor will make that decision, depending on your insurance."

You can't speak, words strangled in your throat. Images assault you. Listless people in white gowns wander in a field with a fence around it; a mammoth, industrial or gothic-looking building looms in the midst—Bedlam, Ancora, Byberry, Greystone Park—places where they hold the mentally ill in captivity.

5:37 pm

Sándor returns with a duffle bag full of your things, just after you begin to calm down. He sits on the edge of the bed and puts his hand on yours. "Do you know what is happening?"

You sniffle, and then answer, "They're sending me away."

"Where?" he says.

"Don't know. A lady came in to interview me."

Sándor waits for you to continue.

"Apparently there isn't room for me yet and they'll let me know after they find out what's up."

Sándor nods. "Did you tell her everything?"

"Nearly."

"It is best to be honest."

"Uh-huh."

"I know you are afraid. Try not to worry."

"Can you stay longer?"

"I will stay until they come for you. Tomorrow I will take Jefferson to my house."

"Thanks, Sándor."

"Please, call me Sanyi. We have been through so much."

"Sanyi. Thank you."

He holds your hand in both of his and you shut your eyes before you cry again.

7:32 pm

The EMTs wheel you from the hospital to the ambulance. From the gurney where you lay, you have to ask, "Um, do you two smoke?"

The girls—they can't be older than twenty-five so they're girls to you—smile and one of them says, "Do you want one? During the day, we can't get away with this. Now it's dark and nobody'll notice." She lights one for you.

"Thanks so much." You inhale deeply and blow out the smoke, relishing the buzz.

They get you settled and you listen to their banter, comforted by the sound of voices.

"After this we're going out. I don't care if it's late," the girl in the passenger seat says.

"We ought to be back by ten. What's open then?"

"The Blue Hog. They have dancing, too."

"Sounds like a plan."

You know they aren't like you; they'll be able to have a beer, maybe two, and sweat it out on the dance floor before they drive home. When you were twenty-five grad school overwhelmed you and drinking wasn't in the picture. Yet. There were plenty of other distractions—mania-driven sex, love triangles and the general anguish that comes from having constant academic deadlines.

You doze.

Chapter Seventeen
Sunday, January 24th
9:37 pm

It's late when you arrive and someone takes your bag. They load you into a wheelchair and take you inside, leaving you outside an office door, which opens after a few minutes. A man gives you papers to sign. You scan the paperwork and notice your patient status says you committed yourself voluntarily. This brings some relief—you're glad you didn't try to argue your way out of going.

A woman soon pushes you down corridors and around corners, across a breezeway and into another building. Now you're in a room where you see people sitting on couches watching television. The woman helps you up; you stretch and yawn. A young man behind a counter with a nametag that says Frank checks you in.

"Let me see. Alexandra McRaven. You're in room 7B," Frank says.

"May I please brush my teeth?"

"We'll get to that. Let's go through your bag."

"I can't just have it?" you say.

"I'm sorry. We have to look for sharps—sharp objects—and shoelaces. We'll give you a plastic bag with your clothes."

"Can I have my purse? I need my phone."

"No cellphones. You'll have access to a phone here, and the payphones. We'll keep your purse locked up. You can keep your cigarettes, no lighter."

"How do I light up?"

"Someone will do it for you."

Thank God.

Monday, January 25th
5:11 am

You're up already. Somehow you got through the night. It's still dark and you walk down the hall to see if coffee is available. A woman named Angie stands behind the counter with her nametag hanging on a lanyard, which rests on the great shelf of her breasts. She's taller than you, imposing, and reminds you of a pinkish-orange refrigerator. Her chic, purple reading glasses glitter with hints of sparkle.

"It's not time to get u-up," she says, her tone sing-songy.

"I'm usually awake at this time."

"Try to be patient. About another hour or so."

You didn't sleep much because your roommate cried into the wee morning hours, making it difficult for you to rest. You don't blame her and would cry yourself if you weren't cried out.

After it's fully light you take a shower and dress. You don't bother to put on shoes. They took the laces out of your running shoes and gave you socks with treads on them to wear. By now it's after six and you walk down the hall to the television room again. Angie looks up from what she's doing and doesn't stop you from sitting on one of the couches. The TV is tuned to a news station and they're giving the weather report. After a while you approach the counter.

"What is it?" Angie says.

"Um, sorry. Can I go out and smoke?"

"You'll have to wait. The first smoke break is at seven-thirty."

"Is there any coffee?" you say.

"There's hot water in the pantry. You can make instant."

"Okay. Thanks."

As you fix the coffee one of the payphones rings. A minute later your roommate runs down the hall. She asks, "Did my mother call? I heard the phone."

"No, your mother did not call. Go back to sleep," Angie says.

"No one ever tells me when she calls and I know she did," she cries, rubbing her eyes. "I need to talk to my mother."

"If you keep this up you're going to lose smoking privileges for the entire unit."

She stops crying and shuffles back to the room.

Outside in the courtyard, a solitary tree stands in the middle with a few benches around it, and they're slushy from last night's wintry mix. You'll try to find a spot under the tree when you finally do smoke.

7:37 am

After the security guard lights your cigarette, you stand off to the side of the courtyard under a slight overhang. You see some guy, burly although shorter than you, approach one of the other patients and ask for a cigarette. They deny him and he comes to you.

"Good morning," you say. You're not able to look away from his forehead, where an X is tattooed in the center, à la Charles Manson's swastika.

"Can I have a smoke?" His army jacket hangs open and you notice there are buttons missing. He wears red and white check knickers—Raggedy Andy pants. You shiver in the cold and think he must be cold, too.

"Sure." You hold out the pack for him and he takes three cigarettes; you keep yourself from frowning because you have to make your one pack last for who knows how long.

He leaves without saying thank you and makes a beeline to the opposite corner of the yard. Another man comes and stands next to you. He has his own cigarettes. Tall and lean with closely cropped salt and pepper hair, he wears jeans and a hooded Princeton sweatshirt.

"I wouldn't give that guy anymore if I were you."

You bristle. "Why?"

"It's like feeding the seagulls at the beach. They take advantage and expect more and more, and then when you don't feed them they get angry."

"Seagulls get angry?"

He smiles, white even teeth striking against the darkness of his skin and orange and black of the sweatshirt. "You know what I mean. What's your name?"

You might be in this place for a while so you don't want to step on toes. "Alex."

"Nice. I'm Jake. How long have you been here? Wait. You're new."

"Yeah—just got in last night."

"It'll pass quicker if you do what they tell you to do."

"How long have you been here?"

"Five days. But I slept a lot when I got here and didn't attend many of their groups."

"Groups?"

"Yeah, things like therapy and art. If you're like me they'll let you go to AA meetings. People from the outside community attend and when you have a couple of days here they let you walk over," he says.

"So, you're an alcoholic."

"An alcoholic with severe depression. That's why I'm here. I've been in recovery for nine years but still struggle with depression."

"It must be difficult to function with both issues," you say.

"I don't mind—most of the time."

You nod as Angie from the desk sticks her head out the door and bellows for all smokers to come inside.

12:04 pm

Other patients stand in a long line, waiting for someone to walk them to the cafeteria for lunch. You don't have the privilege of going anywhere else because you're new. Some people wear sweats like you, others wear jeans and t-shirts and a few still have their pajamas on. Angie walks the line out the door and you watch until the last of them file away. They look normal enough, although despondent and somber—shuffling automatons. There is a heaviness in the air; the lack of windows to the outside world stifles the environment even more.

Your lunch—a slice of ham, string beans and rice with greenish pudding for dessert, which you hope is pistachio pudding—doesn't entice you. Once you cut the ham into small pieces and push it around you don't eat anyway because you have no appetite. You do your best to ignore the pudding.

The lunch line returns and Angie calls for another smoke break. You'll keep to yourself because of the encounter you had with Raggedy Andy Man this morning. You take your coat off the chair, go to the door, and as you walk you see the sun trying to make an appearance. Your spirit lifts. The place under the overhang is taken so get your ciggie lit and move toward the tree.

Raggedy Andy Man follows. This time you brought one cigarette. You won't have to give any up because you left the rest of the pack in your room.

He stands in front of you. "Can I have a smoke?"

"I only have this one," you say, blowing smoke above you.

"I'll take it."

You don't know what to do, so you try and ignore him.

"I'm talking to you," he says, quiet and intense.

"I'm sorry, but—"

"Is there a problem?" Jake says from behind you.

Raggedy Andy Man runs around you and slips a punch at Jake, who dodges it with ease.

As you cry for help, the security guy is already running over.

Jake avoids two more blows by ducking or leaping aside, all the while keeping his hands behind his back. The supervisor restrains Raggedy Andy Man and another security guy runs out the door to help. The second guy grabs Jake's arm and starts for the door. Jake doesn't resist.

You linger in the TV room and your roommate, runs towards the payphone in the corner, shouting, "I need the phone; I have to call my mother." Her voice reaches a higher pitch and now she's crying, "Please! Get off the phone. I need my mother."

Mother.

You feel bad for Maria, but at least she has a mother.

Tuesday, January 26th
4:02 pm

Through the first session with the psychiatrist you cry the entire time. You talk about death and loss—your father, Coach—your lack of a sense of place in this world. The doctor's pleasant face and soft-spoken manner encourage you to speak openly about your suicide attempt.

"You also have a history of self-harm," he says.

"Yes."

"When did this happen?"

"When I was a teenager. It seemed to help—I thought I invented cutting. I hear it's common."

"Yes, it is. People who experience some sort of trauma, particularly as a child, often turn to self-mutilation. What led you to that?"

"My mother died when I was sixteen but…" you say and fight tears before you continue.

"What else?" the doctor says.

"My—my cousin," you sniffle.

"What about your cousin?"

"He touched me—inappropriately."

"Was he older, in or beyond puberty?"

"Yes. It started when he grew all of this hair, his legs crawling with it, his face full of scratchy stubble; I was several years younger. We played Snow White, and he would be the prince and wake me with a kiss. But one day he—"

"You don't have to explain. Did you tell your parents?"

"Not them, not anyone, ever."

"Are you sexually active now?"

"No. Not since Max died."

He waits for you to continue.

"I cheated on him, shortly before he died. I'm just awful. Bad, bad, bad." Then you cry even more.

"It's also common for people with a history of sexual abuse in childhood to act out sexually as adults. Please try not to be hard on yourself."

"How long do I have to stay here?"

"I hesitate to prescribe medication when it's not necessary, and believe the recent circumstances involving so much loss may have led you to harm yourself. I suggest we keep you for a few more days and monitor your progress."

Relief lets your body relax and you stop crying.

The doc clears you for dining privileges, and they move you to a different unit where you have more freedom. They even give you a lighter.

When you return from having a smoke, easier now that you sign out and go outside by yourself instead of waiting to be called, you find your new roommate sitting on the edge of her bed. She has a bandage across her forehead above striking green eyes and wears a hot pink sweat suit, which clashes with her orange hair.

"Hi. I'm Wren. How're you?" she says.

"Fine, thanks. I'm Alex. And you?"

"I'm going home tomorrow, so I'm good. How long will you be here?"

"Doc says a few more days. I hope so, anyway. I'd hate to be in here over a weekend," you say.

"What do you do when you're not in rotting away in a place like this?"

"Do?" you ask.

"What's your line of work?"

"Oh, I—well—don't have a real job. I'm a musician and take work when it falls in my lap. What about you?"

"I'm a glass blower. I make pharmaceutical glass products, test tubes—stuff like that."

"That's highly specialized," you say.

She scuffs her foot a bit. "What're you in for?"

You hesitate. How much do you tell people?

"I tried to cut the voices out of my head—with my husband's Swiss Army knife. He was not pleased," she says.

Your eyes widen, and you keep your jaw from dropping.

"Yeah. He was not a happy camper. He hasn't even been to visit and I've been here over a week."

You want to say something appropriate, but have no idea what. "I'm sorry to hear that," is all you come up with.

"That's okay. He says he still loves me. Hey, want to walk to dinner?"

Your long, audible sigh comes before you can stop it. "Sure."

Thursday, January 28th
1:53 pm

You sit in the front row of the second group of the day, excited because you're going home tomorrow. The room, alive with chatter, grows silent after the instructor hits a small metal bowl with a wooden mallet, its metallic sound stretching across the room as the tone gradually decays. You've heard this before, a Tibetan prayer bowl, or singing bowl, used for meditation, music and different rituals in the East.

The instructor remains quiet until the sound completely disappears. "Today we discuss a meditation practice that will enable us to stay tuned to our surroundings, focus on the moment, and quiet our minds. I'll strike the bowl again. This time, sit up straight, keep your hands on the desks in front of you, and listen to the sound of the bell."

You're aware of nothing but the tone of the bowl, the mellow, steady sound of it and the long length of its resonance. This time everyone stays quiet until well after the bowl stops singing. The instructor says nothing for a while until people begin to stir, and then says, "How much time passed from the moment I struck the bowl until now?"

A man next to you raises his hand. "Five minutes?"

"No. Anyone else?"

Someone from behind you call out, "Fifteen?"

The instructor smiles and says, "Twenty-five minutes."

You hear murmurs from people around you. You don't want to move, and feel lighter, more patient and calmer than you've felt in a long time.

The instructor speaks again. "Your ongoing assignment is to focus on each moment in daily life, stay right there and be aware of your surroundings, take time to breathe deeply and relax." He waves and says, "Until next time."

You stand and stretch, slow and deliberate. Your eyes move to the back of the room; you see Jake and walk towards him.

"I was hoping I'd see you again," he says.

"Jake—oh, my gosh, I'm so sorry about the other day."

"Don't worry. It wasn't you, and it didn't take them long to figure out it wasn't me."

"I looked for you in the dining hall."

"Yes. They suspended my dining privileges for a couple of days and only now moved me over here, off the lockdown unit," he says. "I think I'm going home soon."

"Where's home?"

"I live close by—just outside Princeton. With my meds getting regulated I feel much better, so I'll be glad to get on a schedule. What do you go home to?"

"My dog. I miss him."

Jake smiles. "I miss my kids."

"How many do you have?"

"Thirty-two to be exact." He laughs as your eyes get bigger. "I live in the dorm of a small prep school. I teach math and coach swimming and track."

You rub tears away. "My—the guy I was engaged to, well, he was a coach—high school football—and he taught English."

Jake walks with you, talking as you head for your room. You listen but keep thinking of Coach, and how you have to live life without him.

Friday, January 29th
2:03 am

Wren snores and startles herself awake with a yelp. You're not sleeping anyway so her noises don't phase you, and the snoring reminds you of Jefferson. You smile. Soon she snores again and you hope it's contagious.

As you try to get comfortable and shift your position, you realize you haven't had any alcohol in over a week now. You don't miss it. *Much*. Your head doesn't spin as it did before the stunt you pulled with the poinsettias. You like the sensation of a calm mind; you don't miss worrying, obsessing and fretting over things beyond your control.

Chapter Eighteen
Friday, January 29th
10:32 am

You're checked out of the hospital, papers signed and bag packed. Sándor stands by the front entrance and you hesitate. You're afraid he'll be mad at you for making him drive all the way up here. He sees you and doesn't smile; you don't move for a moment. You give him a terse wave and approach. He lets you come to him and you force yourself to be quiet. He embraces you, then kisses you on both cheeks.

He takes your bag and you protest—you don't want him to lug your stuff around as well—but you're glad to be out the door. The little white pickup truck is parked on the driveway. As you get closer you hear a bark and then long, whimpery howls.

You stop and Sándor turns to you with a smile.

"You brought Jeffrey!"

"I think he knew he would see you today. He paced and wandered the house through the morning."

You lengthen your stride and when you get to the truck you find Jefferson standing with his paws on the window, still barking and howling. Sándor unlocks the door and you're flooded with dog kisses; you hug Jefferson close, and when you get seated he curls up in your lap.

"How do you feel?" Sándor says.

"Tired."

"I have something for you." He hands you a book. "It is *Talking with Angels*. I told you about it a while ago and found this translation."

"Thanks. I'll have a look later." You slip the book into your backpack.

"Are you hungry? Do you want to stop for dinner?" he says.

"Don't you have a lot to do? You've had Jefferson all this time and you must need to get on with your routine."

"Routine is important for you more than I." He pauses and glances at you as he drives. "How was it for you in the hospital?"

"I think I'm a bit less crazy than others from what I saw."

Sándor is quiet again before he says, "What is next for you?"

"Don't know. Back to normal, I guess."

"We are seeing you will allow the Divine Light to heal and nurture you."

"When?"

Sándor laughs. "It will be a lifelong process."

"Sándor?"

"Yes, My Dear."

"Are you ashamed of me?"

He doesn't reply.

His silence scares you and you burst, "I just couldn't deal anymore. I didn't really want to die. I just wanted relief and quiet."

You hold Jefferson close and he licks salty tears off your chin.

Sándor pulls to the shoulder of the road, reaches over and brushes hair away from your face.

You turn towards him and he strokes your cheek with the back of his hand.

"Not at all. But you must be on guard."

"On guard?" you say.

"With the alcohol out of your system your head will begin to clear."

"Isn't that good?"

"Emotions and feelings will become stronger, your memories more vivid," Sándor says.

"I'll be ready for them."

Sunday, January 31st

5:59 pm

You went to church this morning. Nobody asked questions; they were glad you were there. You spent two days sleeping around the clock and don't know what to do with yourself. The condo is even cleaner than when you left. And there's a smell of something you can't put your finger on. Then it occurs to you Sándor may have tidied up in your absence. You haven't bugged him since he dropped you off and now it's time to call.

Sándor answers, "Hello, Alexandra."

"Hi, yourself."

"How are you feeling?"

"All I've been doing is sleeping. I went to church this morning, though."

"How was church?"

"Long, as usual. But it was nice to see everyone. Hey. It feels a little weird in here."

"I took the liberty of cleansing your home. While you were gone, I walked from room to room burning sage," Sándor says.

"Ah, that's the smell. Um, I'm starting to feel—well, to feel."

"Are you anxious?"

"I'm scared. I sleep with the light on," you say.

"Dark entities do not like sage."

"Dark entities. That's all I need."

"You are safe. The fear will diminish as your mind continues to clear."

"Oh."

Sunday, February 7th
8:52 am

"Your voice sounded good last week—you sang well. I was getting worried," Maestro Healey says.

"Thanks. I didn't sing for a while. But I have been warbling lately. My voice feels better, overall," you say.

"It's good to have you here."

"Thanks."

You take your place in the back row. The church ladies who sing alto may not read music well but always show up. The piece Healey chooses for you is lively, what is called a *spiritual*. You've all sung the piece before, but Healey usually plays piano along with you. Today he tries something different.

Healey plays a chord, and you all sing with little help from him. Although the vocal parts are complex with syncopated rhythms and thick textures, the sopranos sing with accuracy and enthusiasm after forty minutes of rehearsal, inspiring the rest of the choir. With a few minutes left to rehearse you stand and do it again, ready to sing in front of the church.

During the sermon, your eyes droop and you close them. You rouse yourself as everyone stands for the Nicene Creed, the Prayers of the People and finally, the Peace. The choristers parade down the stairs and into the church, greeting people along the way. You wipe cobwebs out of your eyes as you lean against the wall waiting for announcements to finish. Then it's show time.

7:06 pm

This is the time of day you usually FaceTime with your father, so you dial Dennis and hope he's around. You know he's busy and don't want to harass him but you're—

"Hello," Dennis says, looking sharp in a lavender dress shirt.

"How are you these days?"

"I miss him. Life continues and I'm busier than I'd like. That's good for me, though. How about you?"

"Without going into the gory details, I've been floundering a bit. To make a long one short, I was hospitalized for a few days."

"Are you sick?"

"Um, no. I'm just—taking things hard."

"Apart from so much loss and grieving, does it have anything to do with your drinking?"

For a moment, you're angry. You don't want to talk about alcohol. But Dennis is one of the few people who witnessed your drunkenness and knows you so it almost feels safe talking with him.

"It was a contributing factor. This Wednesday I'll have three weeks without any alcohol."

Dennis looks down for a moment, then meets your eyes and smiles, gentle and sympathetic. "Are you climbing the walls?"

You sigh. "It's not as bad as I thought it would be—staying away from the package store. And I don't have anything in the house. I'm tired all of the time and sleep a lot, although I make it to church. Today was my second Sunday. I'm not doing much else."

"How'd you sing?"

"I did okay. Healey says my voice is clear—I want to keep it that way."

"Church is probably a good outlet and they're lucky to have you."

"I get paid to be there."

"Enough for a tank of gas a week. Maybe."

You laugh. "That's about the size of it. The choir shook them up today, though, and that was fun."

"What did you sing?"

You sing the opening of today's anthem, "I got a savior in-a that kingdom, ain't-a that good news."

"That's a great one," Dennis says.

"A classic. Even with our small forces we do a good job. And the congregation loves high notes. The sopranos hit them at the end. The church people like to applaud, too."

"That's pretty funny—a High Anglican congregation clapping after the anthem."

Saturday, February 13th
1:02 am

With all the hullabaloo around St. Valentine's Day you want to avoid the grocery store, but have to get some food in the house for the weekend. The store is open twenty-four hours, so you leave the house well after midnight when it isn't crowded.

You groan as you move up and down the aisles; everything is decked from top to bottom with reminders of how you'll spend February 14th alone. Red, shiny hearts and cupids dangle from the ceiling, red and pink crepe paper decorate the deli and you see bundles of roses in bins throughout the store.

You sigh. Coach was always sweet and had fresh flowers delivered to you rather than buying wilted roses from the grocery store. You wander the aisles with your head full of him—his contagious laugh, his sexy golf swing, his ability to draw you out and make you feel comfortable.

You bag the groceries and load the car. As you wait for the traffic light to turn green you stare at the liquor store on the corner and consider. You still can't wrap your mind around Coach's death and drenched yourself with hoo-hah for two months in his absence. Now you don't want to drink anymore to mask the ache.

Once home you find some Bozo parked in your space and you pull into a guest spot. After the engine is off you hear Jefferson barking; he might still have separation anxiety. You hurry to the door with the bags and fumble with the lock.

Jefferson stays under your feet as you put things away and then you fill his bowl. He doesn't touch his food. Something isn't right and you wonder if he's sick; after you're ready for bed he curls up with you as usual.

2:47 am

You wake up startled, sweaty and chilled. Jefferson barks once and then growls—he must be in the kitchen. You'll give him fresh water while you're up. He barks again. "Just a minute, Jeffrey," you say and hang your legs over the side of the bed, rubbing your eyes.

The house seems darker than usual, and you walk to the bathroom, careful so you won't trip over anything. You close the door, do what you have to do and wash your hands, the sound of the running water loud in your ears, something you don't notice when you've been drinking. You smile. You've made it a couple of weeks without alcohol and relief surprises you.

Before you go back to bed you turn off the bathroom light, push open the door and step into the darkness. As you turn the corner a hand clamps over your mouth and his body presses against your back, pushing you into the bathroom. You can't breathe.

"Stay quiet and do not move," says a raspy whisper, hot in your ear.

Chapter Nineteen
Saturday, February 13th
3:00 am

The door closes and the light flips on. You squint, see Zoltán and gasp.

"I had nowhere else to go," he says, his breathing ragged.

You shake your head and exhale, glaring up at him. Then you notice the blood dripping. "What happened?"

He holds up his arm, unwrapping a bloodied towel.

It falls and you stare at his hand. "Where's your—finger?"

"That is not the problem."

"What do you mean that's not the problem? Your finger is missing," you hiss.

"He shot the gun out of my hand and I was not able to find it. Then I heard the sirens. The police will trace the gun to me. I must not be found."

"Gun?"

"My gun, yes."

"Did you kill anyone?" you shout.

He sways, blood dripping from his hand.

"I'm calling the police," you say and turn.

Zoltán straightens up and forces you against the door. "I do not want to hurt you, but will if I have to."

He puts his good hand on your neck. "Then I'm calling your brother," you gurgle as he applies pressure.

"That is the first place they will look. I do not cause trouble for Sándor. If he knows nothing he will say nothing. He does not lie."

"What about me?"

He loosens his grip. You wiggle out of his stronghold and back into the counter so you're trapped.

"I will not stay long."

"You need a hospital. I don't know what to do with that," you say, pointing at his bloody hand.

"You will clean it for me."

"You could get an infection or some other type of grossness. I'm not touching it."

"I will guide you through it," he says.

His face is ashen although he doesn't cry out.

"You should go to the hospital."

"No hospital," he says.

He stoops and pulls a long knife out of his boot, holding it in front of you.

You wince and step back.

"I do not mean harm." He hands you the knife. "Now you must make a fire."

3:31

When you open the bathroom door Jefferson jumps, puts his paws on your waist and licks your hand. You walk him to the bedroom, leave him there and shut the door. Zoltán moves towards the kitchen; you follow. He looks at the stove and you turn the burner to high.

"Not that way," he says, sweat beading on his forehead.

"What do we do then?" you say, hopping from one foot to the other.

"You must make a true fire. The knife will take time to heat," he says, walks to the fireplace and gets the long, iron tongs from where they hang against the bricks. "Hold the handle of the knife with these once the fire burns hot."

You grab some old newspapers and put them under the grill. You have a large bucket of kindling sticks and you spread them on top. Then you go out the slider and bring in three logs.

"Hurry," he says.

Three logs won't be enough so you arrange them on top of the kindling and go out for more. When you come back you find Zoltán in Coach's chair, his injured arm hanging over the side dripping blood on the floor. At least you don't have white carpets.

"Light the fire."

The newspapers burn fast and the flames move to kindling, and then logs. The fire pops and hisses as it gets hotter. Zoltán's eyes are shut and his head leans against the chair. You stand next to it and poke him on his good arm. He opens his eyes but they roll back until they're white, like someone possessed.

"Zoltán. Wake up," you say, raising your voice.

"Alexandra. Sándor and Alexandra," he murmurs.

You ignore what he says and think he'll answer some questions now that he's so out of it. "I have to ask you—"

"Yes?" His eyes return to normal.

"What were you doing with a gun in the first place?"

The fire crackles and he glances at it, then to you again.

"I had a meeting with a rival. I carry a piece always and was prepared. I did not think there would be trouble." He pauses and inhales, pushing the air out like a woman in labor. "As I entered the door of the warehouse, they tried to take me out. They missed—the first time. I took my gun out and fired; they shot it out of my hand. I could not find it. Or my finger," he says with a smile.

"Okay," you say and step back.

"You will place the knife on the flames now."

3:58

The knife is long. You place the metal handle between the pinchers and move to the fire, feeling the heat as you approach, and hold the blade in the midst of the flames. You stand for a while—you're not sure how long—and the blade begins to glow. Over your shoulder you meet Zoltán's eyes; he nods, and then stands.

You don't want to do this.

"Alex. When you put the blade on the wound do so in short bursts. It may take more than one."

You whimper.

"Please. I cannot do it. You have to do it," he says.

He holds his hand out and you lift the tongs, aim and tap the wound once, hearing the hiss of hot metal against bloody flesh.

"Again," Zoltán grunts.

You tap two more times and that's enough.

He stands, about to topple over, holding his wounded hand in the air.

You steady him. He leans on you as you guide him to your room and into bed.

Jefferson dances around your feet and follows you out. Although you want to call Sándor, you don't want him to have anything to do with his brother.

5:17

You're shaking and fretting because you have nowhere to turn and there's a possible murderer in your house. The bedroom door is shut and he won't hear as you power up the Mac. You open Google and do a search for shootings in Atlantic City over the last two days. The first link you see for this morning's Press mentions a man fatally shot at a warehouse downtown, and a gun found at the scene. The gun is registered to Zoltán Vadas, also known as "The Magyar." Police are conducting a search for Zoltán.

A Search!

Monday, February 15th
4:12 pm

You didn't spend Valentine's Day alone; Zoltán slept through the day. The phone rang once; it was Sándor and you were afraid to answer. Zoltán didn't hear it ring. You went to church and fretted the entire time; when you got home you found he hadn't stirred.

Now he's still sleeping—in your bed—and you want to shove him off of it. Jefferson goes about his daily business of sleeping—next to Zoltán—eating and nosing around the yard.

At the foot of the bed where you stand watching them, you worry because Zoltán hasn't eaten a thing and also fret about infection, although any bacteria must have been burned out. His forehead isn't hot or sweaty. You haven't eaten much either and go to the kitchen and warm up some chicken broth.

You pour the broth into a mug and take it to the bedroom. Jefferson lifts his head and sniffs, jumps off the bed and sits in front of you. "This isn't for you, Jeffrey." You put the mug on the nightstand and walk the beagle to the other room and out the slider. When you get back to Zoltán, you see he hasn't stirred so you kick the side of the bed.

"My brother called, no?"

You step back, fear spiking in your gut. "I thought you were asleep all day yesterday."

"And on the day for lovers. He is such a sweet man."

"You need something in your stomach," you say.

"I feel the pain now and need vodka."

"Well, there's nothing like that in the house," you say, testy and irritated.

"You will go get me vodka, no? Take the money from my pocket," he says, turning on his side, exposing the back pocket of his jeans.

"No," you say.

"Very well. I will go myself."

"It's still light outside and I don't want anyone seeing you coming out of my house. Dammit, I'll go." Under your breath you say, "Fucking vodka."

Zoltán takes the mug and sips at the broth. You storm out of the room and let Jefferson in. He trots into your bedroom and you hear him jump on the bed. You poke your head in the door before you leave. "Behave," you say. Zoltán nods and Jefferson smiles and pants, watching Zoltán drink his soup.

4:32 pm

The liquor store is not where you want to go. You have almost a month without drinking and don't want to start again. When you get home, you'll banish Zoltán to the sofa for the rest of the time he's with you and shut yourself in your room.

Vodka. It smells disgusting, and you hate it because it doesn't even work. The number of different varieties is staggering; you go for something cheap. Sweat runs down your neck and you're shaky, afraid you'll drop one of the bottles when you reach for it. You avoid the top shelves, and grab a bottle of Popov. One bottle wouldn't do it for you, and Zoltán is a big man, so you get another one.

You're relieved to be out of there but scared; Zoltán is a fugitive. What if the police come to your house? You'll go to jail because you're harboring a murderer and God knows what else.

When you get to your bedroom you find Zoltán sitting up in bed in his underwear—black briefs—his legs stretched out in front of him. He's still pale, but looks healthy enough. His hair is down, more like Sándor's now, his body lean and muscled. You want to cry.

"You will bring me the bottle?"

You ignore his question for now. "How do you feel?"

"My finger is throbbing."

You go to him and feel his forehead again. "You don't feel hot and obviously aren't cold," you say, your eyes moving quickly over his bare legs and torso.

He smiles. "I am like my brother, no?"

"You are nothing like your brother."

"You will help me draw a bath?"

"No. Do it yourself."

You leave and go to the living room, where you sit on the sofa and look out the window. It's getting dark.

"I cannot open this bottle," Zoltán says from behind you.

You stomp over to him and twist the lid.

6:02 pm

The sound of the tub filling almost drowns out the sound of Zoltán's singing—almost. You recognize the tune, a country music song you've heard before, making you think of your first encounter with Zoltán.

Yuck!

You shake off the memory of that night—the shame of betrayal, the halfhearted desire and the grimy awkwardness of sex with someone you didn't know. And you think of Coach again. He would be disappointed in you and what you've become. What little integrity you had you cashed in for something vile. You stand and pace, feeling so bad about yourself your gut tightens in a knot and now you're doubled over. You're not crying but sobbing, or maybe it's the dry-heaves. You feel sick, and it's not entirely physical. Your mind races, your eyes shifting to the other bottle.

Please, no more.

Zoltán stops singing. The water shuts off and there is only quiet.

Now you're dizzy. The couch is near and you fall on it, burrow into the corner and shut your eyes as tears stream down your face.

Tuesday, February 16th
7:22 am

Jefferson licks your ear. You scratch him on top of his head, smoothing his eyes back as he purrs. The sun blinds you when you open your eyes and you spring off the couch—must've slept all night. The vodka is still on the kitchen table. And you're desperate. Jefferson goes to the slider and you let him out. There's no store open this early in the morning. That'll give you time to think about it. Jefferson finishes his task; you let him in and get the leash.

The day is clear and crisp—lovely—but you don't care what happens. Zoltán is taking advantage of you, and your association with him could destroy your life. You can't call Sándor. There's nobody to help. You think of stopping by Sándor's anyway, so you head for the bridge. Down the street from his house you sit for a while before you turn around and leave.

All the way across the causeway you cry. You know what's going to happen and don't want it to be this way. The Universe has a plan for you, yes, but Sándor can't help and you don't know how to deal with this on your own. Jefferson sits, quiet and shaky, looking out of the corner of his eye at you. You're scaring him and don't have the presence of mind to console him. You sob and scream, "Fuck it. Fuck it. Fuck it."

Chapter Twenty
Tuesday, February 16th
9:19 am

When you're home you walk Jefferson around the parking area. For once, he takes his wiz immediately instead of sniffing around and then drags you to the door. The house is quiet. You take off his leash and go to the kitchen. Jefferson nudges his bowl and you fill it to the top. He attacks the food and chomps with vigor, looking back at you to show how much he loves it.

You pause at the bedroom door, then open it. Zoltán is asleep, so you kick the door shut. "Get up."

He rolls over on his back and stretches. With a casual yawn, he says, "How did you find my brother?"

You start to cry before you can stop yourself. "I didn't see him."

"I forgive you. I must stay on for a while. They are looking for me."

"I can't—I just can't," you say, shaking your head.

He smiles.

"You have to leave, before—"

"Before what?" he says.

Words won't come and you don't know what to say or do so you slap your cheek over and over—hard. Although you grunt at the end of every slap you keep doing it. Zoltán jumps out of bed and tries to keep you from walloping yourself; you're squirmy and he can't get a grip on you. Finally, he smothers you in an embrace and your arms aren't free to keep it up. By now you're wailing. He strokes your hair and murmurs in your ear. It's supposed to be reassuring but makes you sick to your stomach.

"Alexandra, Alexandra, Alexandra."

"Don't call me that." Zoltán saying your full name makes you think of Sándor, and then his caresses make you think of Coach and you melt.

My beautiful man—gone.

Zoltán maneuvers your face towards his, cups your cheeks in his hands and kisses you. The last man you kissed was Coach and you're hungry. You don't resist, sinking into his arms. Your mouth relaxes.

He moves too slowly and you pull at his shirt; then he stops kissing you and stretches your hands above your head, moving to your neck where he sucks gently at the skin.

Then you come to. "Knock it off." You wrench yourself away and Zoltán lets you go, leans back against the pillows and folds his arms behind his head. Your teeth grind together as anger pulsates between your ears. "I want you out of here."

"I see us together. Forget about my brother."

With your fists balled up by your sides you leave the room, slamming the door behind you.

7:31 pm

You can't move, sore from sleeping on the couch. You haven't let the beagle out since this morning. When you make it to the bedroom you find Jefferson sleeping with Zoltán, who shifts his position and faces you, the other bottle of Vodka under his arm.

"He's been out?" you say, eyeing the Vodka.

"Yes. Three times," he says, and takes a big swig.

Zoltán beckons to you with the blackened stump of his finger and you hesitate, standing your ground.

He shrugs. "A few more days," he says.

Your hair, disheveled and damp, sticks to your face and you pull it back. "I'm going to shower then I'll be out for a while."

"It is late, Alex. And you need to eat something."

"So. What."

You feel worse than you did before you went in the hospital, mentally hung over and physically exhausted; you stay in the shower for a long time, scrubbing off your sweat and Zoltán's grunge. You wash your hair twice and it still won't be enough. After you're done you put on fresh sweats and shoes—instead of slippers—and find your phone and keys. You want to take Jeffrey but will feel better if he stays home and guards the house—from what, you don't know—maybe Zoltán, or maybe his minions.

"You should wear a hat over your wet hair."

"Don't pretend to care about me," you snap, and head for the door.

You drive aimlessly in circles and then pull into an empty lot. After rummaging in your glove compartment, you find an old pack of cigarettes and light one up. Smoking forces you to take deep, slow breaths and you relax as you exhale. You make it last a few minutes; your head's as clear as it's going to get. Although you don't want to, you know what you're going to do.

9:03 pm

You treated yourself to bottles of beer this time so you'll drink in style. When you get home, Jefferson greets you and bounds to the kitchen for his food. You set the case on the table, get one out of the box and twist off the cap with the bottom of your sleeve. Zoltán sleeps on the couch; you and the beagle go to your room. You take the case with you, put it on the bed and close the door, hoping Zoltán won't wake up. At this point, almost any music will make you cry so you pop a movie in the DVD player. You haven't seen *The Full Monty* in a while and it might even make you smile.

After your fourth beer, you're flying and enjoying the movie. As you finish each one, you line the empties in a uniform row on your nightstand, evidence of your inability to engage in any normal activity without numbing yourself. You don't want to think about that. After you finish the fifth the phone rings. You jump up to find it, knowing it's Sándor. If you don't answer he'll worry and drive over so you have to get it.

"Hi," you say.

"Good evening, My Dear."

"Ummm, okay."

On the other hand, he knows you're doing it.

"I worry. And I cannot see through the haze of your drunkenness."

Uh-huh.

"Iss, good. All good." You can't wrap your tongue around what to say without saying too much.

"Alexandra. I am not able to help when you do this."

"I'm—don't mean this as an—assault on you. Please don't take it personal—ally."

"Should I come?"

"No, thank you. I'll come see you. When I'm—better." You can't focus enough to string any more words together so you hang up and pass out.

Thursday, February 25th
5:16 pm

You made a large pot of beef stew earlier in the week so you've been able to feed both you and Zoltán. He eats a lot and you'll have to think of something else to cook soon. He enjoys sitting around doing nothing; you don't have to keep him entertained. You run whatever errands you have in the morning and then start on the beer when you're in for the day. You avoid Sándor altogether. He probably thinks you're lost for good and want to stay in your muck. You don't want him involved.

"It is hard that you do not talk to me," Zoltán says.

"Can't you just go?" You walk past him and into the kitchen.

"I will go soon—when the dust settles."

"You've been here almost two weeks. And your brother is worried."

"A few more days."

You may not have a few more days. All you can do is drink to get through it. You can't work on music and don't want to leave him alone for too long. There's no escape.

Sunday, February 28th
11:17 am

Your singing voice is ragged again and you want to make an exit before Maestro Healey approaches you. Father stops you before you can leave.

"We have three more Sundays until Easter," Father says.

"Yes, I know." You glance over your shoulder.

"I would like the children to sing an anthem Easter Sunday, before the adult choir sings theirs."

"Okay. That'll work. I'll begin rehearsing them next week."

You turn away and then Healey stops you. "I'm little worried. Your voice is rough. Do you want me to get someone else to sing for the funeral service this week?"

"Maybe that would be best," you say, lower your head and start to go before he sees your tears.

He touches your arm and you stop. "Alex, is everything alright?"

No.

"Sure." You force a smile. "I've just been tired lately—burning the candle at both ends. You know how that goes—lots to do."

"Don't worry about this week. I'll get a sub for you."

With a nod and a quick wave goodbye you scurry away, reluctant to say anything. His kindness confuses you. When people care you don't know what to do.

You let the tears loose when you're close to home, stop and pull over. Sándor's truck sits on the street near the driveway and you panic. You leave your car and walk to his. When he sees you, he steps out onto the sidewalk and hugs you.

"Someone is parked in your place and I did not see your car so I waited," he says.

You mouth won't open and your throat's tight.

"Alexandra, you are in distress."

All you can do is grit your teeth.

He takes your hand, looks into you and his eyes widen. He pulls you towards his truck and opens the door. You climb in.

You're crying and still can't speak.

"He is here," Sándor says.

You bite your quivering lip, wanting to tell him everything, and you're afraid.

Sándor looks over his shoulder, then at you. "My brother—I saw him in the papers and then Police came to my door. They soon left because I had nothing to say."

Relief allows your chest to untighten. "How come the police don't bring you in—your brother's criminal."

He sighs and says, "I have an arrangement with them. I use my gift to help them with their investigating from time to time, and they do not bother me about Zoltán. This time they have the hard evidence and want to take him down."

"He should be taken down," you say, your voice breaking.

Sándor sits up straighter, as if listening, then his face turns red and he clenches his fists, shaking. "Did he force himself upon you?"

"Please don't be mad at me—he came and was wounded—and I said he could stay for a while—I'm so scared and I didn't want to get you in trouble so I didn't say anything but—"

"You must let me think," Sándor says and bangs a fist on the dashboard, punctuating his words.

For a long while he says nothing.

"Sándor?"

With his head against seat, he huffs. "Alright. I do not know what will happen. I know he is there; my sight is blocked—he has that effect on me—I cannot see into him." He gets out of the truck and comes to your side, opening the door. You step out and he takes your hand, squeezes and then drops it.

When you open the front door, Jefferson runs out and jumps on Sándor, wagging his tail and whining. Sándor ignores him and strides in, looking for Zoltán, who's coming out of the bathroom. Their eyes connect.

You leash the beagle and pull him into a corner. He tries to resist and you hold him tighter.

"I told you not to interfere in my life," Sándor says.

"We are connected to her." Zoltán scuffs a foot, making you think of a bull about to charge.

"She is embroiled but does not belong to you," Sándor says.

"You can have her. She served her purpose," Zoltán says.

Sándor takes a step forward and stops when his brother holds up the stump of his finger. Sándor glances at it and continues.

Zoltán steps back and bumps the wall, holding up his hands. "Peace, brother."

You've never seen them together. You can't look away, full of fear, and you remember Zoltán keeps the knife in his boot. Sándor has him cornered.

"Do not," Zoltán says.

"You will leave now."

"I will leave when I am ready." He reaches for the knife but Sándor pins his neck to the wall. They stand frozen until Jefferson growls. Sándor releases his brother, moves away, and you run to your room, shutting the door behind you.

Chapter Twenty-One
Sunday, February 28th
12:21 pm

Someone—Sándor or Zoltán—knocks on the door, a soft tapping, and it wakes you. You don't want to answer and will cry if it's Zoltán. Jefferson wags his tail, although that could mean anything, and you turn towards the window and pull the covers over your head. Again, knock, knock, knock. With a groan, you fall out of bed.

"My Dear?"

Sándor.

"He is gone," he says.

You open the door. For a moment, your chest constricts; you can't breathe and say nothing.

"I thought that was what you wanted," he says.

You catch your breath and words come. "I'm sorry. It's just been—rough—the last few weeks."

"Alexandra. I should apologize to you. If I had helped the police from the very beginning, you would not have had to endure him."

"How did you get him to leave?"

Sándor pauses and his face darkens. "I threatened to tell his son László about how his mother died."

"You told me drugs killed her."

"It was more than that. Agnes, my sister-in-law, came from Hungary with Zoltán. She did not approve of his actions, his methods of making money."

"So, what did he do to her?"

"It was subtle, but he encouraged her to take the drugs—at first cocaine—and then he exposed her to heroin. She declined swiftly and in her misery, did not care about anything except the fix. Zoltán did nothing. He let her die."

"How awful." Your thoughts lurch away from Sándor and you think of your drinking—how it effects everything you do and throws you into your own a state of misery.

"Alexandra?"

Sándor's voice snaps you out of it. "I'm so sorry for László. I'm glad he has you."

"Yes. I am grateful to have him. Although I fear Zoltán is lost."

You don't know what to say.

"I believe you and Jefferson should come and stay with me for a while. Zoltán's energy is everywhere and you should not remain here. I feel responsible."

"You're not to blame," you say.

"What has happened was meant to happen. Allow me to do what I can."

"Okay."

2:48 pm

"I must attend to György. He has not been out today. It is good you are here, good for him to be social."

"How did he and Jeffrey do while I was in the hospital?"

Sándor smiles. "They were curious about one another; I kept György in his room mostly, but will not this time."

"Where's László?"

"He is staying with his friend Gordy's family on the mainland this week. That will be nice for him."

"He's safe then. Good."

You have enough clothes to last over a week, your laptop and plenty of food for Jefferson, who seems delighted to be here. With Sándor's indoor pool you also brought your bathing suit. And you might even write some music.

Jefferson knows the house but takes his time sniffing around. You have to put his leash on to get him to come to your room. He looks over his shoulder toward the kitchen as you walk. You shut the door behind you and let Jeffrey explore.

There are drawers for your things, a desk for your laptop and the bed is covered with a duvet, soft and squishy. You kick your tattered slippers off and smile as you unpack, remembering the sunken bathtub. You draw a bath and Jefferson sleeps, curled up in the corner of the bathroom as you relax in the tub. The steam from the hot water makes you woozy; you'll have a nap after you're done.

8:29 pm

You awaken to the sound of Jefferson's whining; you hear that high-pitched whistling noise dogs make when they're upset. You reach out in the dark and scratch his head. He stops whinging and you turn on the light. Groggy, you step out of bed and wonder where you'll find a place to walk him.

Sándor's standing at the stove when you get to the kitchen. He wears an apron over his clothes, white with black lettering, "Love the Cook!"

"Did you rest well?" he says.

"Yes, thanks. But Jeffrey has to go out. Any strips of grass around here?"

"Not many. I take him on the beach. You will not go alone."

"I'll be fine—"

"No. I am almost done and will go with you."

You're relieved and throw a coat over your pajamas. Sándor removes his apron and grabs his overcoat. Jefferson wags his tail and grins, his tongue hanging over the side of his mouth.

It could be a lot colder; the temperatures reached sixty degrees during the day; now it's in the mid-forties. Tomorrow promises another mild day. The night is clear and you, Sándor and Jefferson walk up the ramp to the boardwalk and then out to the beach. The moon gives off enough light to navigate by. Jefferson's leash is retractable and you let him wander as he likes.

You haven't felt this calm in weeks. With Sándor, you also feel safe. Jefferson is persnickety about the water. As the waves move in slowly over the sand he sniffs at the foam but won't get his feet wet. You walk a few blocks and then turn around. The beach is deserted, although every now and then you hear the treads of a lonely jogger passing by on the boardwalk.

"Are you hungry?" Sándor says.

You haven't thought about food until now and your stomach growls. "Actually—what's for dinner?"

"I have asparagus and will make us omelets if you like. You want Swiss cheese?"

"Perfect."

You reel Jefferson in and he leads you and Sándor up the stairs towards the house. When you're inside Jefferson follows you around the kitchen as you follow Sándor. You remember when you were a young girl how you stuck close to your mother as she busied herself in the kitchen, to see how she did things and to be near her.

Mom and dad—both gone. Coach—gone.

You're able to take care of yourself, but have trouble caring whether you do or not. You realize you're not moving anymore, and instead stare out the window into the dark. Queasy in your gut, the world shifts and you relax again, so much that you feel yourself sinking.

"What happened?" you say as you realize you're lying on the couch with Sándor sitting on the edge of it. The beagle nuzzles your ear and paws at your sleeve. You try to sit up but can't get your bearings.

"Stay there for a moment. You need to eat something. I will bring it to you."

Sándor returns with an omelet and a glass of juice. You don't speak until you eat and he takes the dishes to the sink.

"That was weird," you say.

"It is what happens when you undergo a psychic attack."

"From what?"

"Not what, but whom."

"Zoltán," you say.

Sándor nods. "I did not realize—did not see it coming. But then I gave him a shock."

"A shock?"

"Yes. I sent my brother the white light. I knew he was probing you only after you fell to the floor. He will not bother you now."

Sándor sits on the couch and wipes his brow, closing his eyes.

"Is something wrong?" you say.

With his eyes still shut, he says, "I cannot see into Zoltán but was able to send the burst of light. It is tiring, making the energy to connect with him."

"Do you know where he is?"

"I sense he is far away. Perhaps in the city where he has connections. He will vanish into the woodwork for the time being, and may return. We must be aware."

Friday, March 4th
7:02 am

You've been sleeping throughout the night and for much of each day for most of this week. Sándor left a pitcher of water in your room as well, so you make sure to keep hydrated, flushing out the toxins from your experiences with Zoltán.

Well-rested, you dress and head for the kitchen with Jefferson. Sándor sits at the table having tea. When he sees you, he stands and pecks you on both cheeks. "Good morning, My Dear."

"Morning. Ready for a walk?"

"A quick one. I must get György to his room."

"Why quick?"

"Today I will go to your place for the cleansing. You should remain here. Do you need anything?"

You consider. You've been using Sándor's laundry room and have fresh clothes. "I think Jeffrey could use more food. But that's all, really."

"That is good. I will refill his bucket."

You look around for Jefferson and see he's sniffing the air by the large cage in the corner of the room beyond the kitchen. The parrot flies to a higher branch, remains quiet, but hops from one foot to the other. The beagle whines and stands on his hind legs.

"Jeffrey. Sit," you say.

He sits and lets out one, short bark.

György scratches his chin and says, "Sit."

"György! You can say sit!" you say.

You look at Sándor and he laughs. "He is a great mimic. I think they like one another."

He rinses his cup.

"Sándor?"

He turns towards you. "Please, call me Sanyi."

"When will I be able to go back home?"

"Freeing your house of the negativity will take time. I will do another cleanse next week and we shall see."

3:37 pm

You sit at the piano improvising, head clear and thoughts free. For the time being you're healthier than you've been in months, relieved you're not drinking.

Sándor comes through the kitchen door. His arms are full and you jump up. "Do you need me to carry something in?"

"No, I have only one more trip. Please, continue."

"I was just starting to worry."

"We will talk when I return," he says.

Now you're self-conscious and can't play, although happy Sándor's back. The animals have been quiet this afternoon but now that there's more activity they're awake and having a barking match. Jefferson lets loose a bark and György echoes, the same short, percussive timbre. You have to smile.

"I have something for you. Three guesses," Sándor says.

You play along. "Um, is it a chocolate milkshake?"

"No, not this time."

"A duck-billed platypus."

He smiles and shakes his head. "One more guess. But I will give a hint: Feet."

"Purple toenail polish."

A bag sits on the chair and Sándor pulls an oblong box out of it.

"Shoes?"

"Not just any shoes."

You open the box and take out a soft, black leather slipper with black fur trim. "Oh, they're nice."

"Much needed," he says with a frown at the slippers you're wearing.

You laugh. "But what's wrong with the ones I have?"

He rolls his eyes. "Try them on."

They feel delicious on your feet and fit perfectly. "How'd you know what size?"

"I measured your feet."

"Ha!"

"My Dear, there is something else." Sándor takes a smaller box from the bag.

The package is from Coach's sister. "What's this?" You open the package and read Joan's note, which is brief but lovely, then take out the pocket watch you gave Coach for his birthday the year before he died.

"Please, may I see?" Sándor says.

You hand him the watch and he reads the inscription on that back out loud. “For My Coach, With Love Always, Your Alex.” He gives it back to you. “It is beautiful. I sense his love for you.”

You sniffle and nod. “I miss him.”

“Of course you do. You are a part of one another and always will be.”

Sándor keeps his distance and lets you cry—good—because you don’t want to be placated anyway.

Chapter Twenty-Two
Thursday, March 17th
6:12 pm

For the two weeks you've been at Sándor's house, you keep things as normal as possible. László came home after the weekend and although he stays in his room a lot, you take meals together. You and Sándor have an understanding you won't mention Zoltán in László's presence.

Although you're still shy around László, you try and make conversation. "What are your favorite subjects?"

He takes another bite of potatoes. "This year I have Geometry and Algebra and they're okay. I like Biology the best. Except—"

"What?" you say.

"Except I don't like studying plants. They're boring. I like it when we dissect things."

"Ew. The creatures they make you dissect smell. I think it's the formaldehyde."

"It's not so bad. It's like doing surgery. That's what I want to be—a surgeon."

"A noble pursuit."

László shrugs and continues eating.

When you're finished you clear the table and do the dishes. Sándor has a client soon and you want to get hold of Dennis. As you dry the last glass, Sándor approaches now that László is in his room. "I stopped by your place today."

Fear pools in your stomach.

"All is well. I checked your mail."

"Anything good?" you say, swallowing. He says everything is okay but you wonder.

"See for yourself." He hands you a large envelope and leads you to the couch where you both sit.

You take the mail out and find a few catalogues and other junk mail. "Wait," you say, and pull a letter out from between a couple of bills. The crisp envelope is from a preparatory school in the Philadelphia area. Addressed to Dr. Alexandra McRaven, it looks enticing. You open and read over it.

"Wow."

"What is it?" Sándor says.

"They want to commission a children's opera—grades seven through twelve—on a story of my choice. Hey, this is huge."

He smiles. "I knew good things would begin to come to you."

"This'll be great for me. I'll call them tomorrow, first thing."

"Alexandra, while you are welcome to stay here for as long as you like, your home will be ready tomorrow, after the final cleanse."

You shudder. "I don't know if I'm ready to go back there."

Sunday, March 20th
6:56 pm

You texted Dennis the other day to see if he was able to FaceTime with you. He wasn't available then and you set up an appointment for seven o'clock this evening. On the dot of the hour he calls.

"Hey," you say.

"Hey, yourself." He whistles. "You look great! What have you been doing?" Dennis peeks over your shoulder and then says, "And, where are you?"

"I'm at a friend's house for a couple of weeks. I needed a change."

"It's done you good. How was church today?"

"Fine. The children are singing a little *Gloria* I wrote for them and they're getting it. Adult choir is good, too. What are you doing for Holy Week?"

"I thought I'd lay low and take a break from school. I had some nice invitations—people trying to keep me from getting lonely. Honestly, I'm okay."

"Want to come down for Easter? I'm going home tomorrow."

He pauses for a moment and then his face brightens. "You know what? That sounds fine. As long as I can skip all the church gloom—until Easter Sunday."

"I hear you. You can relax or do whatever you want."

"That's a good idea—I'll check the flight schedule. There's probably something out of Boston into Atlantic City."

Tuesday, March 22nd
6:31 pm

Sándor drops you off and you wave as he drives away. Jefferson sits on the concrete, waiting to see what you'll do. "Okay, Peep. Let's go." You haven't been to the condo since the day Zoltán left and that was three weeks ago; rather than delaying you open the door and walk in. You don't smell anything, then notice the flowers Sándor left on the table, an array of yellow roses, baby's breath and a few daisies.

Sweet.

You're free until tomorrow morning when you have to pick Dennis up from the airport. If you feel like it, you'll poke around the internet and think about that children's opera.

Jefferson settles in and falls asleep on the deck by your chair where you read through unopened mail you shoved in a drawer when Zoltán was with you. Once business is taken care of, you don't know what to do. It's dark and you go inside.

Later, after you change into your pajamas and crawl into bed—

SLAM!

—you think of drinking.

There's nothing in the house; if there were you'd be at it. Sándor took all that crap out, cleaned everything from the kitchen cupboards to the bathroom to the dust on your nightstand and the cobwebs behind the stereo cabinet. You're tempted to go out and get something. But you find the phone instead and call Sándor.

"Hi. Sorry," you say.

"I was hoping you would be alright," he says.

"I don't want to bother you. I don't know what else to do."

"No bother. I am glad you called. Do you want me to come and get you?"

"I would love that, except tomorrow I'm supposed to have company until Sunday and I'm not ready to be here at all, even with Dennis coming."

"You may bring Dennis to my house, and then stay until you are ready," Sándor says without hesitating.

"Really?"

"Alexandra. I have a vision that includes Dennis. There is room for him. We are seeing goodness, renewal and knowledge that you will get through this."

"I feel like I'm being such a baby—"

"It is not expected of you to do it all alone. Come right over."

You sigh, relieved.

Wednesday, March 23rd
10:02 am

Dennis's flight is on time. He spots your car. You pop the trunk before you get out and run to embrace him.

"I'm so happy you're here," you say, and put his bag in the trunk. Dennis carries another bag as well, small enough to keep with him. "Nice man-purse."

He smiles and says, "A gift from your father."

"Yes, that's like him. Sporty and stylish."

As you drive you fill him in on what's been happening, except for your adventures with Zoltán. "And—"

"What's up?"

"Well, I haven't been drinking. Lately."

Dennis is quiet, and then elbows you, lightly in the ribs. "Your father would be proud."

"I hope so." You pause. "Sándor's house is amazing. And he's quite something, a gentle giant."

You feel his eyes on you as he says, "How did you meet him?"

"We had a fender-bender, or as he says, our cars collided." You leave it at that.

Thursday, March 24th
7:32 pm

Holy Week usually creeps you out—the sparse attendance of the evening services, the darkness of the church without daylight, the solemnity of the sermons and the overwhelming sacrifice God made for us. *For God so loved the world He sent His only begotten Son.* You did nothing to deserve that and your own sordid iniquities stagger you. Being in church this week is a reminder.

You were here last night as well for the Tenebrae service, although there wasn't any music. Tenebrae, meaning darkness, is the time where the lights and candles are gradually extinguished throughout the service, leaving one final candle symbolizing Christ. The last candle is hidden at the end, the apparent triumph of the forces of evil as the light has faded. Tonight, Maundy Thursday, gets to you even more, especially at the end.

Father called this afternoon, asking you to volunteer for part of this evening's ritual during the service. You agreed since you're not singing. There aren't many people in church and the congregation sits in the first few rows of pews. Following Jesus's command to love and serve one another, Father washes the feet of a few of the parishioners.

Maestro Healey and one of the sopranos from the choir sing a duet version of *Panis Angelicus* as Father moves down the line cleansing feet, coming to you last. You had a long shower before church but still worry about how your feet smell. He takes his time washing them, kneeling before you—gentle and gracious. Long melodic lines of the voices singing echo through the church, beautiful and poignant. Father's humility throughout the slow pace of the cleansing ritual moves you, somehow driving home the possibility that you also are deserving of grace as a child of God.

The church is quiet as Father and his acolytes strip the altar. The red hanging banners are taken away; a black cloth now covers the large crucifix on the wall. During the part of the service when chimes ring three times, you only hear three sharp, wooden thuds, evocative of the barrenness of a world without the Light of Christ.

After the service, you drive slowly home; gratitude and relief fill the void in your gut, relaxing and giving you a sense of peace. For once you feel a part of things, not merely attending church because it's your job, and now you have friends to rely on and share things with, give to and care for.

The garage door opens and you sit in the car for a moment, just saying thank you. When you come through the kitchen door you see Dennis, Sándor and László sitting in the living room laughing, Jefferson sleeping at the foot of György's cage.

And it is okay.

Friday, March 25th

11:04 am

The entire week has been mild and today is the warmest yet. You have a few hours before you're due at church for the Good Friday service, so you head to the beach with the rest of Sándor's current household. Dennis walks in the sand with Sándor and you and László have a catch with the baseball. As usual, you're afraid of the ball; László is patient when you let it drop in the sand next to you.

"Are you hungry?" you shout over the wind, running towards László.

"Sure," he says.

"Good. Go get your uncle and Dennis then."

Lunch consists of bread and cheese, grapes and apples. Dennis tells anecdotes about your father and his unorthodox methods of teaching, his flamboyant ties and high-top sneakers. You've heard it all before and smile as Sándor listens. Even László asks questions.

"What was weird about the way he taught?"

"Alex's father believed a hands-on approach to learning and teaching was the only way. He wanted his students to be musicians, not merely scholars," Dennis says.

"That sounds fair," László says.

"That's why I spent years struggling with the piano, and now I sort of play my own music or at least accompany myself, when I have to," you say.

"You should have heard the piece Alex performed for Cormac's memorial service," Dennis says.

You blush.

"She sang and accompanied herself, and the piece was a dance with Latin words—not Latin as in salsa, but churchy words she set to music. People loved it."

You look at your watch. "Well, speaking of churchy, I've got to head back."

Sunday, March 27th
9:17 am

The children are ready for today's Easter Sunday service. For some reason, they're not as reluctant and sing louder than usual. This makes it easier for you. Adult choir rehearsal is also no problem; the choir knows the music because it's an old standby, Beethoven's "Hallelujah" from *Christ on the Mount of Olives*. You don't have to follow the music and keep your eye on Healey.

During the sermon, you listen rather than space out. Father's message of embracing diversity touches you, bringing hope for better times ahead. Christ died for all of humanity, without discriminating.

At the end of the service the congregation stands for the final hymn and Father and his entourage recess to the back of the church. "Alleluia! Christ is risen!" Father says, and the congregation returns, "The Lord is risen indeed, Alleluia!"

Your spirits lift so much you even stay and mingle. You turn red as some ladies from the choir make a fuss over your new outfit—a blue dress with fuchsia-colored flowers. For once, you don't wear dark colors. And you don't have to force yourself to smile.

You see Sándor and Dennis in the front of the church talking with Father, who is more animated than usual. When he sees you he says, "Great job with the children, Alex." He turns and moves towards other parishioners, waving at Sándor and Dennis as he leaves.

"Yes, My Dear. Your children's anthem was beautiful and they sang well," Sándor says.

"I'm impressed you get them to learn it on such short notice," Dennis says.

"They learn by ear—I spoon-feed them every note. A grueling process but it works."

You and Dennis drive separately from Sándor because you have to take Dennis to the airport. There's a bit of traffic on the Expressway and you talk as you drive.

"I like him very much," Dennis says.

"Who?"

"You know who I mean. Sándor. He's good for you."

"Yes, well, I'm not entertaining that thought at the moment."

"You don't need my permission, although you have it."

"Thanks."

You get out of the car, hug Dennis and watch as he checks his luggage. "Take care of yourself and keep in touch," you say.

"I will. Remember what I said. I give you permission to be happy."

"Uh-huh. Safe flight."

On the way to Sándor's you think about what Dennis said. It never occurred to you that you don't allow yourself to accept anything good unless it bites you on the ass. Then you think of Coach. He was one of the good things—right in front of you, lost in the shuffle of your insecurities.

Too late now.

Chapter Twenty-Three
Tuesday, March 29th
2:02 pm

The weather is mild for late March. The first thing you do when you're back at the condo is open the slider and pull the screen door across, allowing fresh air in. Crocuses and daffodils poke through the soil along the fence. Jefferson noses around the hemlock trees.

This time you're comfortable on your own turf, although you haven't been here through the night yet. You think about the children's opera and rifle through your books. There are rows of them on bookshelves and stacked in corners of closets. Jefferson scratches at the door; you let him in and continue searching.

The books are not organized and you don't know what you're looking for but it'll hit you when you see it. Something public domain is best so you won't have to write for permission to use the text. Fairy tales appeal to you, especially those of the Brothers Grimm, but you can't find your collection.

You come across a section of Jane Austen novels, followed by the Brontë sisters. The book Sándor gave you after you left the hospital rests between Anne and Emily—where Charlotte should be—an English translation of *Talking with Angels*, transcribed by Gitta Mallasz. Now you're sidetracked; you turn the front cover over where Sándor's handwriting stands out. In a beautiful, angular script his words say: *Dear Alexandra. May you read the Dialogues with courage and wonder. Yours, Sándor.*

After you scan the introduction and preface, you're intrigued enough to keep going, and slow your pace. From the beginning, chills course through your veins. You pause, go to the slider and switch from screen to glass door. Then you throw on a sweatshirt. None of this helps and the shivers continue as you read more. The words frighten you.

Luminous beings spoke to Gitta Mallasz and her three friends in a time of universal upheaval, a time when guidance was needed desperately. Only Gitta survived to transcribe the Dialogues. Her three friends died in Nazi concentration camps. Your small world consists of problems largely of your own making.

The phone rings. You hesitate, but need to talk—to anyone. "Hello?"

Nothing.

"Hello?" You hang up, startled, knowing it was Zoltán.

By now it's dark. You're frightened and the phone rings again.

You answer and wait before you speak.

"Alexandra?"

"He called—"

"I am sorry, My Dear. I was the one who called."

"Why didn't you say anything?"

"The spirits whispered to me as you answered. They told me something of great importance was happening to you."

"I was out-of-my-mind scared to begin with and you made it worse."

He ignores your testy comment. "We are seeing things happen as they should—everything you experience and feel—all meant to carry you through to the next."

"That's not comforting."

"What has you disturbed?" he says.

"I'm reading that book you gave me and can't put it down. I don't know what to think of it."

"If you are reading it now you are meant to."

"It's speaking to me and freaking me out," you say.

"Yes, and no," he says.

"What's that supposed to mean?"

"The angels allowed Gitta Mallasz to transcribe the conversations to reach people who were and are willing to benefit from them."

“These are not fluffy, white-robed angels we’re talking about here. They’re cranky and impatient, not what you’d expect from divine beings.”

Sándor laughs.

“It’s not funny.”

“Be gentle with yourself, My Dear, and keep reading.”

Thursday, March 31st
9:31 pm

The *Dialogues* scare you. They also inspire. As you lay, purple and yellow colors flash before your eyes, and you think of the crocuses and daffodils that will bloom in the back yard. *Flowers*.

After the deaths of Coach and your father, you let your commitment at the hospital slip away and now you’re ready to continue again. Optimism is a concept foreign to you. But that’s what you feel. You think you can sleep, then your thoughts leap to the children’s opera.

Of course, the one book you want to find, you can’t. You keep looking and finally resort to your Kindle. The book is cheap, too—Chaucer’s *Canterbury Tales*. You also order a good translation so you won’t have to fight with the Old English text. You browse through the stories into the early morning, and come to the “Nun’s Priest’s Tale.” As you read the story of Chanticleer the proud cock and his foe, Sir Russel the fox, you hear music in your head and know this is the one. A fable with talking animals along with the singing rooster who is susceptible to flattery will make an exciting musical setting for children.

Wednesday, April 6th
7:16 am

Rain is forecast for later today. The first thing you do is take the spreader out of the car and flood the grass with seed. Then you tackle the flower beds on the south side of the church. With the winter's mild temperatures there are weeds everywhere. You pull them from the roots and move to the front of the church, a much larger area. There are bushes, rhododendrons and azaleas, along with a few small evergreens—plenty of room for flowers.

You're filthy and the progress you made tidying the beds satisfies you. The bags full of weeds are heavy; you lug them to the car and hoist them in the back. Then you see Father Marcus.

"Hi, Alex. Looks wonderful. I'm happy you're here. Thanks."

"You're welcome. It's fun for me. I plant at my house but there isn't room for much, so this is great."

"See you Sunday."

You smile. With a flat of flowers in each hand, you carry them to the plots with a spring in your step, and start planting along the south side. You dig holes for the pansies, a hardy flower that will withstand cooler temperatures. The splashes of purple and yellow color around the church delight you.

Monday, April 18th
4:38 pm

There's a café near Sándor's house, where you're meeting him today. The wind blows in small, cool gusts; you find a table outside in the sun. You're a few minutes early and he's always precisely on time. He approaches and when you stand to greet him his eyes move over you from top to bottom.

"You look wonderful, My Dear. It is good to see you." He hugs you and sits when you do.

"I clean up okay. Finally had my roots done, too." You giggle and lean forward so he can see the top of your head.

"Very nice." He smiles. "How are you coming along with the *Dialogues*?"

"I got away from them—distracted by the children's opera. I'll get at it again."

"All in good time."

"Are you going to have coffee or tea?"

"I think I will have a chai. May I order for you as well?"

"How about if you let me get them this time."

He nods.

You're having hot chocolate to celebrate feeling good and when you take the mugs outside you find Sándor talking with a lean man in a suit. Your eyes are drawn to the holster under his open sports jacket and you step back in the door. After a few minutes, the man leaves and gets in a car parked across the street.

"What was that about?" you say.

"That is Logan. He is a detective I have worked with before. We spoke of my brother."

"Is he around?"

"The world is small, but there are places for him to hide. This time I will do what I can to help the police if he appears."

You shudder.

"Will you be alright? I know you have concern," he says.

"Yeah. Are you free this evening?"

He sips the chai and looks over his shoulder. "I am." He hesitates.

"What?" you say.

"Would you like to come over for a swim?"

"Um, I could for a while. I don't have my suit."

"You left it hanging in the shower. It is washed and ready."

You drive the few blocks to Sándor's and he walks over and meets you. Your hands shake as you drive, not only for fear of Zoltán. This will be the first time you swim with Sándor. Your stomach flips like you're on a rollercoaster, and the sensation is not unpleasant.

You change into your suit and take a robe off the hook in the bathroom, draping it over your shoulders. The house is warm and when you get to the pool area it's even warmer, maybe too much. Between that and your nerves you sweat. The water will feel good. Still wearing the robe, you sit on the edge of the pool and dangle your feet in the water.

Sándor waves as he comes through the door wearing blue swim trunks with yellow polka dots, a towel hanging around his neck.

So. Goofy.

Your fear and modesty vanish. You realize how comfortable you are, more so with Sándor than—then you think of Coach and your mood shifts. You remember saying the same thing to Coach weeks before you lost him.

"What is it?" Sándor says.

You pull the robe tight around your shoulders.

"We do not have to swim."

"No, I'm okay, it's just—"

"My Dear. I am here for you." He moves to the corner of the room and picks up a giant beach ball. "If you want to go in let us play a catch," he says, and bounces the ball on the floor.

You smile in spite of yourself.

He stands in the deeper water and you remain in the shallow end as you throw the ball back and forth to one another, chatting. At one point, you dunk your head because your hair is in your face and you want to let the force of the water push it back. You come up sputtering and coughing, alarming Sándor, who moves towards you.

"Are you alright?" he says, patting your back.

"Ugh, sorry. I got water up my nose—gross."

A long strand of hair sticks to your face. Sándor reaches out and smooths it behind your ear. His hand lingers against your cheek. You feel yourself turn red and glide away to shallower waters. The moment is over and you continue bantering about simple things.

Dumbass.

Tuesday, April 26th
7:06 pm

For several days, you avoid Sándor. Time flies from one moment to the next as you work on the children's opera early every morning and attend to the gardens at church. You're in a groove and feel grateful, although your thoughts flit from Sándor to Coach, to Zoltán and back to Sándor again. Although you want his affection, it's too soon.

Eventually you break down and call. "Hi, it's Alex."

"It is good to hear from you."

"Are you busy?"

"Not at all. My client just left," he says.

"Are you around this weekend? I finished the book."

"Brava, My Dear. Will you come Friday evening? László is away on a class trip for the weekend. I have to call on someone in the afternoon and will be home for dinner."

"That sounds fabulous. If you want, I'll come early and rustle up some chow."

"I do not know what to rustle up chow is."

"Make dinner."

"Ah. That is good. Please bring your copy of the *Dialogues* and we will discuss."

"Great," you say, relieved to hear his voice.

Friday, April 29th
6:07 pm

Sándor isn't home yet. You park, take the groceries inside and decide to walk the beach while it's still light and there are plenty of people around. Dinner won't take long to cook. You picked up a few fillets of salmon, potatoes, green beans and ice-cream.

Your step quickens and slows along with the music in your head, the melodic lines from your opera for children. You also hear the blaring brass fanfare from *The Rake's Progress* and want to compose something similar for the piano introduction to your piece, which you haven't worked out yet. For now, the vocal parts come to you without any accompaniment.

You walk south and turn around after twenty minutes. In the distance, you see Sándor's house, impressive as it sprawls toward the boardwalk. Beyond, the hotels of Atlantic City rise out of the evening mist. Your stomach churns with excitement.

The boards are deserted, surprising, because it's a mild evening. You climb the steps, cross and move down the ramp while you hum melodies in time to your steps. You open the car and click the remote, careful to lock the car again before you go inside.

In the kitchen, you steam the green beans and boil the potatoes. When they're done boiling, you stand at the counter and mash them, singing out loud, "Here am *I*, CHAN-ti-cleer." You baste the salmon with olive oil and take fresh dill, scattering it over. The house smells fishy as it bakes so you light a few candles.

You're happy—dinner will be delicious, ready soon for you and Sándor, and your opera is taking shape. You sing louder, "CHAN-ti-CLEER!"

You mash harder as you sing in your opera voice, high and resonant, add milk and sour cream to the mix, and the potatoes become less lumpy. You're dying to try them but make yourself wait for Sándor—you open your mouth to sing another phrase and arms circle your waist, clasping below your breasts. Surprised, you lean into his arms, closing your eyes.

This time, you're going enjoy it.

You tilt your head and reach your arm back to stroke his hair. But there is no hair. One of his arms moves over your breasts and stops at your neck. You're confused and try to pull away. He won't let you.

Zoltán.

"Sándor will be here any time," you stammer, opening your eyes.

"Be quiet," he hisses.

Shit.

You're able to see him when you cock your head to the side. Zoltán is clean-shaven with the exception of a closely trimmed beard that forms a ring around his mouth. If he didn't look like a gangster before he does now.

"And where is my brother?" he says. "You are very cozy with him."

"He'll be here any second," you gurgle.

The kitchen door opens and Zoltán spins you around.

"You will leave now," Sándor says with menace in his voice.

"Give me the painting."

"I do not have it."

"Where is it?" Zoltán shouts.

"Safe in a vault."

"You lie. It is here. Go and get it else I will snap her neck."

Sándor steps forward. Zoltán releases his hold and slams you into the refrigerator. "Do not come closer," he says and pulls a gun out from where it was tucked in the back of his pants.

Sándor stops.

"I will find the painting myself," Zoltán says, the gun aimed at his brother.

You whimper from where you lean against the refrigerator.

Zoltán glances at you and Sándor takes another step.

"Do not!" Zoltán says.

Sándor ignores him.

Zoltán fires the gun and the force of the hit hurls Sándor against the wall, where he slides to the floor, slow and wide-eyed.

Chapter Twenty-Four
Friday, April 29th
7:17 pm

You open your mouth and nothing comes out. The parrot screams. Your head's heavy and your face hurts. You dart your eyes towards Zoltán. "Fuuuck!"

"Stay with him. Do not call 9-1-1," he says, and moves into the hallway.

You rise and stagger to Sándor. Blood seeps through the shirt on his upper arm. His eyes flutter. He moans and tries to lift his head but can't. You get up and find a pillow from the couch, place your hand under his head and slip the pillow under. He opens his eyes.

"What do I do?" you say.

"Wait. He will soon leave," he says, breathing labored. Sweats beads on his forehead. You run and get a damp cloth from the bathroom.

In the hallway, you bump into Zoltán, who carries something wrapped in a sheet. "Wait twenty minutes. Then call 9-1-1," he says.

"You shot your brother!" you say.

"He will survive. The wound does not threaten his life." He reaches out and caresses your chin. You cringe, and see blood on his hand—your blood.

"See someone attends to that," he says.

When you get to the kitchen Sándor's trying to get up.

"What're you doing?" you say, and help him sit against the wall. "He said to wait but I'm calling now."

For once you remember where the phone is. You take it out of your coat pocket and dial 9-1-1. "My friend was shot...Alexandra McRaven...One Baltimore Street...my cell is…shot in his upper arm…he's about fifty…yes, breathing and conscious…the guy who shot him is gone…thank you."

7:46 pm

You shiver. The ambulance pulls away, and you step into the police car, eyeing the house over your shoulder as you turn onto the street. Yellow police tape stretches across the garage door. There are still a few policemen at the scene making their investigation.

The sound of sirens grates on your nerves and you hold your hands over your ears. Blood continues to drip from your nose during the ride. Maybe you'll know what's up with Sándor when you get to the ER, and suppose they'll clean you up and take your statement.

The officer guides you through the door to a desk, and you give them your information. You only have to wait a few minutes before you're moved to a private room. The officer sits in the corner while the doctor attends to you. There's a crunch as he sets your nose, and you whine. The bleeding stops; now you're aware of the pain as they place bandages on your face.

"What about Sándor? Will he be okay?"

The doctor ignores you.

The cop, who stands by your bed, says, "What is your name, and what is your address?"

You tell him that and everything else.

10:02 pm

Your nose is numb and you can't breathe through your mouth because it's parched, and your stomach's upset so you can't drink any water. When you try and breathe through your nose you can't get enough air. You inhale in short, sniffly gasps, like you're crying, although you're not. All you feel is relief. The cops are letting you go. You're going to see Sándor.

When you walk through the door you see Sándor's left arm in a sling. He opens his eyes.

"Are you in pain? Did they get the bullet out?" you say.

Dumb questions.

"The bullet went in the wall in the kitchen. The police must have it."

"So, it got stuck in the wall, and not in your arm."

Sándor exhales slowly. "Yes, thank God. It was a shock. Not much pain yet."

"I'm so sorry," you say, as you drag a chair beside his bed and sit.

"No. It is I who am sorry. Are you feeling okay, except for your face?"

You put your hand to your nose and wince. "Yeah. I'm scared. And I have to get back to Jeffrey."

"How will you get home?"

"One of the officers says he'll take me to pick up my car and follow me home, so don't worry."

Sándor tries to lick his lips but they're too dry.

"Do you need water?" you say.

He nods and you pull the bedside tray closer to him and hand him the water, which you help him drink through a straw.

"Better," he says. His eyes start to close and he snaps them open.

Before he sleeps, you remember to ask, "What about László?"

"I was able to call Gordy's family. When he returns Sunday from his class trip they will keep him for the week."

Sándor dozes again.

"You should sleep," you say, and take his good hand.

He squeezes, loosens his grip and drifts off to sleep. When you get ready to leave you pause, turn around and go back to

Sándor. You bend and kiss him on the forehead. He smiles and snores with his mouth slightly open, his breathing less labored.

11:14 pm

Your hands, unsteady on the wheel, shake as you drive. When you get to the condo the policeman walks you to the door, and you hear Jefferson's howls.

"Thanks for following me."

"You're welcome, ma'am. Standard procedure," he says.

As soon as you open the door Jefferson flies out, running figure eights in the parking lot. It's late and you don't want to yell so you let the beagle's energy run its course. After a minute, he calms down. The officer drives away.

Jefferson never pees in the house but that's the first thing you smell. There's a pile, too. You go to the kitchen where he's already nudging his bowl, and you give him fresh water and food.

You walk the rooms, searching with your nose for messes. Once you finish cleaning, the condo smells like laundry detergent and you're satisfied things are tidy enough.

You're unsteady and finally cry. You flop on the couch and Jefferson sits on your foot, leaning against your leg as you sob. Fear wells up like a blob of dread in your gut as your thoughts turn to Zoltán. He must be far away by now—he's not stupid. They're looking for him. When you calm down you put pajamas on and fall into bed, the beagle nestled in your arms.

Saturday, April 30th
12:36 pm

You were up earlier to let Jeffrey out but went back to sleep, dreaming of pirates; Zoltán and Sándor drink bottles of rum, slur country music songs at their wenches, and laugh in their stupors, sloppy and lewd. You wake in a panic and—

SLAM!

Although it was just a dream, the idea of Sándor acting like his brother terrifies you—and you still smell the rum. You hate rum. Unlike whisky, you can't drink it straight; there's a sickening sweetness to it. But if you mix it with something that has an edge to it, like a diet soda, it goes down smooth without tasting like baby aspirin.

You take care of the beagle and shower before you head out the door. It's too cold to take him with you so you kiss the top of his head and go. Sándor probably wonders where you are—you said you'd see him in the morning and it's after noon. On the way to the hospital you pass the liquor store and don't stop. You're eager to see Sándor and that saves you for now.

The hospital room is warm. Sándor sits in a pool of sunshine, propped up with pillows. He smiles out the window until he looks at you and sees your expression.

"Alexandra, you are not well."

"I'm fine—just tired."

"There is something else, I think," he says and gestures to the chair. "Please, sit."

"Really. I'm good."

He lets it go.

"When can I spring you out of here?" you say.

"Tomorrow. I am taking antibiotics and will continue when I am home."

"What do they give you for pain?"

"I take nothing for that."

"You're amazing," you murmur. If you'd been shot, you'd cash in on every opportunity to feel good if you feel bad and feel better if you feel good.

"Alexandra?"

Then you think of drinking again. You'll stop and get some hoo-ha as soon—

"Alex."

You turn towards Sándor and shake off the clutter in your head. “I’m sorry. I was spacing out.”

“Will you be able to take me home tomorrow afternoon?”

“Sure. Can I come after church?”

“Of course,” he says and pauses. “Be careful.”

He even knows when you’re thinking about drinking.

“Yup. I’m okay.”

After you say goodbyes you leave without looking back and drive to the liquor store.

5:17 pm

Yo-ho-ho.

You’ve already thrown up twice, once in the hamper, and the second time you made it to the bathroom. You continue to drink the rum-punch concoction. Jefferson left the room a while ago; the smell is bad and you’re wallowing in sorrows, loud and strident. The phone rings and you don’t answer. They don’t leave a message. A few minutes later it rings again and you answer.

“Yeah?”

“What are you doing, Alex?” Sándor’s voice is stern.

“Nothing?”

“I cannot help if you do this.”

“Um, I di-dint ass for help.”

He sighs. “I want you to pour it down the drain. Now, while I am with you. The act of ridding yourself of it will help you.”

“Um, no.”

“You are making yourself sick again. We cannot move forward if you are too ill to continue.”

“Continue what?”

“Our path—together,” Sándor says, his voice low.

Then you cry and end the call. You don’t want to continue anything.

Sunday, May 1st
10:50 am

Somehow you make it to church. It hurts your nose to sing. You do it anyway. For the anthem, the choir sings "Be Not Afraid," from Mendelssohn's *Elijah*. The nagging fear still assaults your stomach and you're hung over. You arrived late so the church ladies wouldn't question you about your face with its bandages. You'll scoot out the door as soon as you can after the service.

11:58 am

You walk the halls on the way to Sándor's room, sheepish, dragging your feet to prolong the time before he scolds you. *You deserve it.* With a deep breath, you walk through the door and find him dressed. He smiles and relief floods your gut.

"Hello," he says.

"Hi. Is it time to go?"

"Almost. Someone will come with a wheelchair and take me."

"How about if I pull the car up front?"

"That is a good idea," Sándor says, just as an orderly comes in to take him downstairs.

You excuse yourself. There are other people in the elevator, and you feel stifled so you stand in the corner, stiff and quiet. Sándor is fine with you, although you wonder if you'll hear about it on the way to his house—the drinking—how you can't be alone under stress without your hoo-hah.

But he says nothing.

You're both quiet as you drive, and don't say much as you go through the garage into the house.

"Can I make you some tea?" you say.

"Yes, please."

You boil water for the tea and chat as you wait. “Do you need anything?”

“No, thank you.” He winces as he tries to stretch his wounded arm.

“At least it’s not a cast. That would be itchy.”

“Yes. There are stitches; they come out next week.”

The kettle whistles. You pour the water and after the tea steeps you carry the mugs to the deck. Sándor stretches on a lounge chair and you sit beside him.

“What’s next?” you say.

“I have to call my clients and make a schedule for the week. And you, My Dear?”

“I have to do something productive. I thought I’d write this week, maybe work on the requiem or the children’s opera.”

“That would be good for you. Use the gifts you have been given.”

“Uh-huh.” The tea is cool enough and you gulp it, and say, “I’m sorry about the painting.”

“Ah, yes. The painting.” He smiles.

“What?”

“That was not the painting.”

“The one Zoltán took?”

“Yes. Long ago I had a copy made.”

“Where’s the original?”

“As I said. Safe in a vault.”

You’re quiet and then say, “You don’t lie, do you.”

Sándor turns to you and shakes his head. “No. I do not lie.” He looks towards the ocean; the wind blows his hair around his face. “I am ready for a rest,” he says.

“Good. You need it.” You bring the mugs in the house and put them in the sink. When you turn around you find Sándor close behind you and for a moment you’re trapped.

“Alex.”

You wait for him to speak.

He doesn't say anything.

You're about to slip away from him and he pulls you to him with his good arm and kisses you hard.

He finally pulls away.

You're in shock until he breaks the silence.

"That is a promise. Please. Go and find your way. I am always with you."

You don't know what that means, and talking is inappropriate. You're unsteady and stumble towards the door. When you look back Sándor's watching you, and then he turns and moves towards the deck.

Chapter Twenty-five
Monday, May 23rd
8:02 am

Music notation paper sprawls on the desk and you hop from there to the piano and back as you find the proper musical notes and gestures, then write them down. There's no sense in scoring the requiem for anything other than piano, chorus and soloists. You'll never have an orchestra at your disposal. And you're happy with that.

You love that you're sketching the music rather than composing at the computer. This forces you to savor the journey of writing without rushing to finish for a deadline.

Lux.

Lux aeterna.

The open-sounding chords accompanying the words "light eternal" rise slowly; the chorus ascends with them and sustains, high and floaty, as the chords descend again. You indulge yourself and sing the opening soprano line of the movement. Your voice is clear, and you observe the dynamic markings and sing the high notes as soft as you can. Jefferson lifts his head as you sing.

The children's opera isn't done, but it's not due for another year. Your need to finish the requiem presses you and each day you continue until it's almost completed. The writing flows and you're grateful for this burst of creativity. You write music for almost three weeks, from before dawn to midmorning. That's what keeps you going, that and Sándor's kiss—a promise.

If you behave.

Sándor's busy with clients and you only speak on the phone. You're comfortable, with only occasional thoughts of Zoltán. For the first few nights you sleep with the condo lit up to soothe your fear. Now you're able to rest with the certainty he's nowhere near.

Yet, you worry.

Composing keeps you distracted and out of trouble. You don't want to think about the time when you won't have a project to keep you in line and you can't imagine—

The phone chimes.

"Hello?"

"Hey, how are you doing?"

"Dennis! I'm well enough today. How about you?"

"I'm okay; it's cold for May."

"That's too bad. We've been having nice days recently. So, what's up?" you say.

"I'm wondering if I might borrow the Berlioz signature?"

"Sure. What're you doing with it?"

"A colleague asked me to join his lecture and give a presentation on the *Symphonie Fantastique*, one of your dad's specialties."

"Absolutely. I wish I could come and see. It'll be a nice tribute to dad."

Sunday, May 29th
8:44 am

You're early and hope Healey's already there. You finished the requiem the morning before and have a score for him. Butterflies swirl in your stomach, nervous eagerness rather than angst. It took almost a month to finish the piece, fleshing out and improving sketches you made years ago.

It's warm and you get out of the car just as Healey pulls into a parking space. You wave and he smiles. With score in hand, you stand by his car.

"What do you have there?" he says.

"I've been working on something and I'd love to run it by you."

"Come in and we'll talk before everyone gets here."

"Thanks," you say, and follow him to the choir room.

Healey opens the score and takes his time with the first movement. “Alex, this is beautiful, but the music’s agitated in parts and challenging for soloists and chorus.” He pauses and looks further. “I love how the men harmonize in low thirds while the women have ethereal, high lines over them.”

“Thank you. Do you think any of it’s doable?”

“Can I keep the score for this week? How about if I call you when I have a chance to review the entire thing.”

“That would be great. Please take your time with it.”

You move to a seat in the back row as other choristers arrive, your head high and your stomach calm.

Thursday, June 2nd
4:02 pm

Jefferson races down the beach and stops to inspect a horseshoe crab. The smell hits you first and then you see it’s dead. The beagle licks a piece of seaweed stuck to the crab’s spikey tail, and moves on. He doesn’t need a leash; it’s the only beach around where dogs can run free.

You enjoy Jefferson, smells of ocean and sand, and the steady roar of salt water. Quiet and still, you’re aware you have a month without hoo-ha; in March you had some time, but only because Sándor held your hand through it.

You cry often, as memories of Coach and your parents surge in your mind. You see Coach’s boyish face and hear his laugh, and your body still aches from the loss. You’ve fallen too many times, resorting to hoo-hah to stifle the pain; the urge to imbibe can slam you anytime. You’re almost forty-seven years old—time to grow the hell up.

When you’re home you feed Jefferson and listen to the messages on your cell phone. The first is from Sándor. You listen as he babbles and your spirits lift. The second is from Maestro Healey. “How does All Soul’s Day 2016 sound to you?” his voice says. The message is brief but you get the point and bounce on your toes. He wants to do your requiem—too good to be true. You can't wait to tell Sándor.

He doesn't answer, then calls back in a few minutes.

"My apologies. I was showering with György. He likes his bath."

You picture the stream of the shower pouring on Sándor's wet hair, his muscled body sleek and soapy, the parrot fluttering about, squawking and chattering happily with—

"My Dear?"

"Oh! Sorry. You know what? Take a guess!" you giggle.

"What is it?" he says.

You can hardly contain yourself. "Three guesses."

"You rescued another dog."

"Nope. But that's a good idea."

"You—are traveling to Fiji."

"Ha. But not without you."

He's quiet for a moment; you can tell he's smiling. "You finished the children's opera."

"Close," you say, breathless. "It's the requiem. I finished. And Healey wants us to perform it on All Soul's Day this year!"

"Wonderful. I look forward to it."

"How's your arm," you say.

"It is beginning to lose the scabs and scar. It looks worse than it feels, still sore to lift things, although much better, thank you."

"I'm glad you're on your way. How's your, um, schedule?" You're hesitant and don't want to come right out and ask.

And you don't have to.

"I would love to see you. Do you want to come by tomorrow, and bring Jefferson?"

You almost cry but restrain yourself and say in a low voice, "It's been a while."

"Yes. Now is a good time."

Friday, June 3rd
3:51 pm

Your stomach flip-flops with excitement because you haven't seen Sándor since early May. Jefferson knows where you are when you turn onto Baltimore Avenue and he barks, wagging his tail. "Alright, Peep. We're here."

The combination to open the garage door is still in your head; you open it and get the beagle. After you go around the pool Jeffrey trots down the hallway ahead of you and noses the kitchen door open. Sándor stands by the stove stirring something in a huge pot. The beagle bounds at him; Sándor stoops to hug him.

Then he moves towards you and kisses you on both cheeks.

You blush, thinking of your recent daydreams.

Sándor grins.

He must know all the gory details. Sheesh.

"I am making us a fish soup. It is windy this evening."

Jefferson's under Sándor's feet and you get a bowl and put some food in it, which he ignores. Sándor almost trips over the beagle and says, "Jefferson, you must want your food."

"He wants our food," you say.

He continues to stir the pot with his back to you; the jeans he wears fit him well, quite nicely, in fact, and the way his broad shoulders fill out the Henley shirt—fetching to say the—

"…and I thought we might take our dinner on the deck in spite of the wind, perhaps have a fire in the ring…"

No. He is nothing like his brother, not in any way, from his appearance to the way he treats others with compassion and dignity and—

"Alexandra?"

"What?"

"I have a surprise for you. We should make plans now if you like the idea," he says.

"Sounds intriguing. Can we talk over dinner?"

5:19 pm

You're suspicious of the soup and eat it anyway—for Sándor. The different textures of the ingredients are weird, and you don't like fish much in the first place. You keep yourself from wrinkling your nose.

"This is delicious," you say, swallowing.

Sándor laughs. "I know you do not prefer it but it is full of nutrients you need to keep you strong."

"So, now that I don't like your soup, what's this surprise?"

"I have a client who owns a Bed and Breakfast in Stockton on the Delaware River. He invited me to stay for a few nights. I would like to take you for a weekend if that pleases you."

"Road trip! B & Bs are nice but most of them don't allow dogs. Or parrots."

"I see. I was not thinking of Jefferson." He pauses, considering. "I will speak with my friend, Nathan. Would you mind?"

"Not at all. And I can chip in and help with whatever we need."

"Chip in?"

"You know, contribute financially," you say.

"That is good of you, but please. This trip will be—how do I say—on me?"

"You got it. Thanks. That'll give me yet another thing to look forward to."

Tuesday, June 21st
11:02 am

Every day you take Jefferson to the dog beach. You have to bribe him with biscuits to get him back on the leash, and he eventually comes. When he was younger you never would've gotten him back because of his wanderlust. He's more mellow now. The daily routine of writing, beach with Jeffrey, and more writing gives you a sense of peace as well as purpose, and the tears come less.

Sándor's picking you up later to look at camping supplies. He wants to give László a tent for his birthday so he can camp with his football buddies. You smile as you think of Sándor, and wonder how much he really does see. He certainly knows when you're not being good.

While you're waiting for Sándor the phone rings and you hesitate because it's a New York City number. Then you think you might have a request from your publisher so you answer.

"Hello?"

"Alex, this is Sam."

You feel generous so you're nice to him. "Hi, Sam, how're you?"

"I won't keep you. I have news."

"Everything still the same with the contract?"

"Yes, and more."

"What?"

"We want to publish your requiem but feel you should score it for chamber orchestra instead of piano."

You're flabbergasted.

"Are you there?" he says.

"I don't know what to say."

"You can start by thanking me."

"Thank you—I'm just surprised, that's all."

"Don't be. It's a good piece."

"I never thought you'd have interest, but sent it anyway to let you know what I've been up to."

"Well, we'd like to have the larger-scale version soon," he says.

"I'll get right on it. I'm so grateful."

"Does this mean you'll have dinner with me?"

"No," you laugh.

"A valiant effort for naught."

3:07 pm

Sándor arrives. You say goodbye to Jefferson, lock the door and hop in the little pickup truck. "It smells good in here."

"Yes. I had it washed and cleaned inside this morning."

"Where are we going?" you say, as he turns a corner sooner than you expected.

"László is at his friend Gordy's house. He will come with us and we will shop for his birthday."

"It's his birthday? How old, fifteen?"

"No. He is already sixteen. He had a late start in school early on—because of ill circumstances."

You don't push him to explain. "So, he'll be driving next year."

He brightens. "Yes. We go for his driving permit soon."

László opens the door and says, "Hey, Alex."

"Hello. I heard it's your birthday."

"Yeah. But not till a week from Thursday."

"You'll be driving soon and that's got to be exciting."

He cracks a rare smile. "If my uncle will let me."

"Sure, he will," you say, elbowing Sándor.

You sigh as you drive by László's high school, where you imagine Coach's enthusiasm for teaching and coaching still lingers in the English classroom and on the football field. You try not to think of Coach; your thoughts have been turning to him lately, and you feel bad because a part of you doesn't want to move on. You shake off the memory and focus on the present.

The sporting goods store is overwhelming—everything an athlete or sportsman could want, from bug repellant to generators to fishing supplies and guns, which make you nervous, even BB guns. Sándor goes straight to the camping section and László stands by the fishing rods and picks up a shiny red and black rod.

"Do you fish?" you say.

"No, but I always wanted to. I used to ride my bike to the bay with a net and string and go crabbing. That's all you need."

"I went fishing with my mom and dad when I was a child, never in the ocean, though. May I get you this rod for your birthday if you like it?"

László smiles. "Really?"

"If it's okay with your uncle, sure."

You find Sándor looking at tents. "How's it going?" you say.

"This is a big tent. It should be enough for László and a few friends."

The thought of Sándor crouching around underneath the tent roof, stooping because of his height, makes you smile. "When is László going camping?"

"Before football practices begin, just before his birthday."

"Ah. Sándor?"

"Yes, My Dear?"

"I'd like to get László a fishing rod for his birthday. He seems excited about it."

His face darkens.

"What's wrong?"

"I am worried he will go off by himself to fish somewhere and—"

"We could go with him, or I could. And only in daylight."

"I do not see that something bad will happen. But I worry about him, and you."

"Don't worry. Everything will be okay."

"Alright. You may do it."

László chooses a black and blue, heavyweight ocean rod and you buy the black and red one for yourself, along with appropriate fishing accessories. Sándor buys the tent, lanterns and batteries for László's camping trip and has them reserved for delivery to his house.

You chatter with László on the way to the truck, carrying your rods. This is the most excited you've seen him in a while. The three of you discuss plans for his birthday. You'll meet him for your first fishing expedition on the beach in front of Sándor's house that day.

Thursday, June 30th
5:29 am

Before you get to Sándor's you stop at a bait shop. There are a few men hanging around talking. They ignore you. When you ask no one in particular what sort of bait to use for surf fishing they grow quiet and stare. You stand your ground.

One of the men slides off a chair and looks you over before saying, "There's squid, there's blood worms and there's lures. That's what we got today."

"What's best?"

"I'll give you squid and the worms, if you want. And the lures. You got rigs?"

"Yes. I have—top and bottom rigs. Forget the lures. I'll take some squid and worms, enough for two people to fish all morning. And one of those plastic thingies, you know, to hold your rod."

"You mean a ground spike?"

"Yeah, that's it," you say with defiance.

You watch as the man who helped you prepares the worms. Your eyes widen as you see them ooze into the plastic container. They don't call them blood worms for nothing. You grab some plyers and a good knife.

As you pay for the goodies and leave, one of the other men snickers.

Sándor's in the kitchen having coffee when you arrive. You already had coffee and want more. He hands you a cup and pecks you on the forehead.

"Where's László?" you say.

"He is on the beach setting up chairs." He sits. "Thank you, Alex. I did not think of this fishing idea and it is good for him."

"My pleasure."

You're quiet as you finish the coffee.

"I will watch from the deck for a while and then come down later," Sándor says.

You left the gear in the garage; after you collect it you head for the ocean. There's a land breeze but close to the surf the bugs shouldn't be too bad. László sees you and waves. Your hands are occupied so you smile and he runs towards you.

After you're settled in a chair László rummages through the tackle box and finds what he needs. You rig your own rod and when you're done you open the bag with the bait. He opens the lid with the squid first. It's still frozen and he sets it on the sand in the sun. Then he opens the worms.

"Yuck," he says.

"My thought exactly. Hopefully the fish will love it."

You both laugh as you bait the hooks.

The weight on the end of your line makes casting easy and satisfying. You stand about thirty paces down beach from László and watch as he lets more line out. He's a natural fisherman. You enjoy the ritual of casting and reeling in slowly, then casting again. After a while you sit your rod in the stand and jog to László. As you reach him the first thump-thump of the day tugs at his line. He reels, pulling the rod back, and you see the end of the line skip along the water with a crab dangling from the hook. He yanks the rod back and the crab flies off.

"For a minute there I thought we'd have crab imperial for dinner!"

"Don't worry, if we don't catch any fish this morning Sanyi probably has a backup plan."

You laugh. "We could order a pizza."

You're squeamish but you get a blood worm. It wiggles on your palm and leaves a residue of bloody slime; you imagine it squeals curses at you in its worm-language as you pierce it with the top hook. On the bottom hook, you attach a thick lump of squid. You wade into water up to your knees and cast. After a few minutes, you start to reel the line in and there's a strong tug, so strong it pulls you out. "László!"

He puts his rod in the stand and runs to you as you fight with the whatever-it-is on the line. You don't want to let more out, afraid it'll break. Handing the rod to László, you step away from him so he can reel it in. He backs up a few paces, gently pulling the rod with him. Then he reels it in more, walking into the surf. The fish is a big one, and struggles to take the rod, and maybe even László, with it into the ocean.

"Whoa!" he says, and reels until the line drags the writhing fish onto the sand in front of you.

"What is it?"

"Don't know," he says.

"Is it edible?"

"I have no idea. We'll ask Sanyi."

11:02 am

The house smells delicious. Sándor didn't make it to the beach, was busy in the kitchen baking László's birthday cake. He hugs you. "How did the fishing go?"

"Wait till you see it."

He raises his eyebrows. "And who captured this delicacy?"

"László is the man of the hour," you say, just as he walks into the kitchen.

Sándor applauds and László says, "It landed on Alex's line."

"Yeah, but I couldn't reel him in."

Sándor knows how to clean a fish, but says, "You both caught it. You two can clean it and I'll cook it."

It's near noon and you excuse yourself to go home, shower and take care of Jefferson. You'll return later for dinner. You hum as you drive, perplexed because you're happy, and for once the feeling isn't fleeting.

Chapter Twenty-six
Wednesday, July 20th
9:43 am

You scored the requiem for chamber orchestra, basically one of every instrument. The musicians who play woodwinds also double on their auxiliary instruments—flute on piccolo, oboe on English horn, clarinet on bass clarinet, bassoon on contra. Plus, you have brass quintet, strings, timpani and two percussionists. They'll make a lot of noise when your music gets loud.

The only thing left is the dedication and you know what to do. You want to tell the world how much you loved him, how wonderful he was, to you and others. You want to shout about his sense of humor, his passion for teaching and his affectionate nature. In the end, you keep it simple and type *To Coach* on the title page. After you have a cry you send the digital score to your publisher. Then you put it behind you.

Friday, July 22nd
11:56 am

You're nervous.

The doorbell rings.

"Hello, My Dear," Sándor says.

"Hi, yourself. I brought too much stuff—didn't pack the computer though—I need a break."

Sándor picks up your bag, puts it down, takes a step towards you and says, "Alexandra."

"What?"

He hesitates, pulls your hand to his mouth and kisses your palm.

You shiver as your pulse races and your body heats up. Nobody ever kissed that side of your hand before—delicious.

He draws you to him, holding you close. "You must know I love you," he whispers. His body tenses.

"What's wrong?" you say.

"I will try and be patient."

You caress his cheek. "I don't think you'll have to wait too long."

"Shall we go, then?" he says.

"Yes, let's."

Sándor drives your car. The first thing you do once you get going is shove the compact disc into the player. You're elated to begin with, and the playlist of Bruckner scherzos and allegros keeps you hopping; you laugh as the scherzo from the *Eighth Symphony* booms through the speakers. You wiggle your butt and dance in your seat. The energy from Sándor's smile fills the car, egging you on to sing along with the music, "BUM…bum bum bum bum BUM…bum bum bum bum BUM…bum bum bum bum BUM."

It takes two hours to get to the Delaware River area. Once you're off the highway, the road winds along the canal. In some places, you see the river through the trees. Your stomach's fluttery with excitement as Sándor turns up a hilly road and shortly after you see the inn on the left, an old farmhouse set back off the road. The driveway brings you to the other side of the house and you park along a fence. Sheep graze in the field beyond the fence and lift their heads when you pull in.

"Do you want to come with me while I go and find Nathan?"

"Sure."

As you approach the house a man comes out the back door. He's much shorter than Sándor and their embrace is awkward with one man stooped and the other reaching up. Sándor drapes an arm around Nathan's shoulders and moves to you.

"Welcome to the inn. And you are?" Nathan says, and hugs you, but not without a smile at Sándor.

"Thank you. I—" you say.

"Forgive me. This is my dear friend Alexandra."

"Please, call me Alex."

"Well met, well met," Nathan says.

"Thank you for having us," you say.

"You're welcome. Come with me. The Garden Cottage is this way. It's newly renovated, an old carriage house from the 1860s. It's the only place we allow pets but you didn't bring the dog," Nathan says, turning to you.

"I'm sure he's moping in the kennel."

"You'll have the cottage to yourselves then."

"We will manage," Sándor says.

The cottage is spacious and luxurious with a king-size, four-poster bed. There's a cozy sitting area with a couch under stained glass windows. The bathroom has a double whirlpool tub and also a separate, oversized shower for two.

You're antsy. Sándor and Nathan won't stop talking, and the sense of expectation in your gut is all-consuming. Then Sándor's eyes lock with yours. You move to his side and he takes your hand. They talk for another minute; you're only aware of your hand in Sándor's clasp.

Their conversation ends and the room is quiet, awkward and thick with tension. "I'll let you two get settled," Nathan says.

After Nathan leaves Sándor turns around and leans his back against the door. He closes his eyes, exhaling audibly. When he opens them, you move toward him as he strides forward and scoops you into his arms. He's still kissing you when he sets you on your feet and tries to pull your t-shirt over your head. You're frantic to get him undressed and fumble with the zipper of his jeans. You stumble over one another until you both figure out it's quicker to undress yourselves.

You don't make it to the bed. Sándor pins you to a wall, his hands moving through your hair to your breasts and your bottom. All the pressure—months of restraint—unleash. His body, slick with sweat, presses to yours with violent energy. As he pushes himself through you he moans, "Alex. Alex. Alex." You know he's getting close and you're almost there, too. These moments exhilarate and terrify you—the urgency, the driving need.

You love it.

Sándor's final groan muffles into your shoulder. He shudders. You stroke his great mane of hair and relief you haven't felt in ages washes over you. He lifts his head and faces you; you kiss his face, his eyes, his mouth.

He carries you to the bed, and after another long kiss, you both sleep.

8:31 pm

It's almost dark when you wake up. The growling of your stomach makes you giggle and Sándor stirs. You nuzzle his ear with your nose; he kisses you and says, "Hello, My Dear. How are you feeling?"

You return the kiss. "I feel so good I'm not sure how to handle it. Except I'm hungry. Are you hungry?"

"I am."

"There has to be someplace open at this hour. Let's call for a pizza."

Saturday, July 23rd
8:01 am

The sound of knocking startles you; unable to move, you fall back asleep. Then kisses wake you—not the usual slobbery, slurping of dog kisses—but the deep, invigorating kisses that can only come from someone who loves you. You open your eyes. Sándor stands over you wearing one of the robes supplied by the cottage. It's too short for him and barely ties in the front. You smile.

"Breakfast is here," he says.

"Mmmm, wow." You pull the sheet from the bed around you because you're naked, stop by your overnight bag to grab something to wear and head to the bathroom. You'll need a shower, but you're hungry now.

You both eat quietly, with only murmurs of pleasure as you sample the different breakfast items. With your belly full you head for the shower, pausing to kiss Sándor on the way. He pulls you to him and you both end up in the shower.

You finish before he does, towel off and find something to wear. Once you're dressed, you take a quick look in the mirror because shorts make you self-conscious. You've lost weight since you stopped all the hoo-hah. For once you think you'll get by without fretting about what your butt looks like. You don't care, anyway. And neither will Sándor.

He comes out of the shower with that too-small robe on, drying his hair. "Did you rest well?"

"God, yeah. I needed it. What's the plan?"

"I have an itinerary," he says as he dresses.

"You're so organized. I'm fine with anything we do."

"Do you want me to tell you or make a surprise?"

"Surprise me," you say.

"Good. I think you will like it."

"Perfect."

"Come, my dear," he says, taking your hand. Then he pauses. "You look ravishing."

"Must be the shorts."

1:36 pm

You stroll with Sándor through the meadow, hand in hand. An ocean of July wildflowers decorates the landscape. His nose is buried in a book; he raises his head to point something out to you or identify a wildflower. Each time you come to a new specimen he consults the book, reading as he walks. He often loses his balance and you laugh as you steady him.

"And this one is butterfly weed," he says, pointing to a plant with little orange flowers and thin leaves.

"How about this one?" You touch the small, red bunches.

He browses through the book. "Ah, that is the cardinal flower."

"Ooh, this one's pretty."

Once again Sándor looks through the book. "St. John's Wort—actually, it is called shrubby St. John's Wort."

"I like the bright yellow of it. Isn't that a remedy for depression?"

"Yes."

"Ah."

The wildflower preserve offers a variety of trails, from flat, wide paths through the meadow and around the pond, to more rugged and hilly terrain. Sándor slides the book into his backpack and finds the map of the preserve. "Let us see the pond next," he says, and embraces you.

You leave the meadow and move toward the pond nearby. Dragonflies flit across the path to and from the water; birds trill and chirp, a cacophony that delights you both. Once in a while you hear a plop as a bullfrog jumps in.

Before you tackle the more difficult trails you go to the visitor's center for a pit stop. It's crowded so you get in and out of there fast. When you're outside you see Sándor looking at the map. People have to skirt around him and he's unaware of it. You take out your phone and snap a photo of him looking intent and focused.

"Hey. What's next?" you say.

"Are you ready for something more strenuous?"

"Sure. Could use a workout—I'm a mess."

He kisses your forehead. "You are beautiful, My Dear."

You blush and look away. "Couldn't be. I'm all sweaty and gross."

"You are healthier than I have ever seen you."

"Thank you." You blush as he puts his arm around your waist.

"We never had a chance to discuss the *Dialogues*," he says.

"Yeah. They spoke to me."

"What do you take from them?"

"One of them asks the Angel why she is tense, and the Angel answers: *because of self-importance*. I don't know what that means, except I think I have to get out of my own way."

"Yes, my dear. Wonder comes only when you forget yourself. When you are tense you do not grow."

"The Angel also said the only place to find joy is beyond the old me."

"So, you let go of the past and try not to take it with you," Sándor says.

"What I valued most—drinking—now I value least."

"That was a burden you were accustomed to, you were used to its weight."

"I'm trying to slough that off."

"And you are doing well."

You follow an easy path until you hear the sound of water rushing over rocks and come to an old stone bridge with three arches. After that the ground is uneven and although you stick to the trail, you slow your pace as you climb higher. Sándor is behind you and when you turn around you see he stopped, holding his shoulder.

"What's wrong?" you say.

He glances down the hill and says, "Nothing. My shoulder aches today."

You know it hurts where his brother shot him. Sándor never mentions it and you don't want to think about it either. "How about you take the lead and set the pace."

He's quiet as you trudge up the ridge. When you reach the top, you lean into one another as you sit on a big rock and have some water. The view is spectacular with the creek in one direction, the stone bridge you crossed, and far beyond, the meadows, alive with a wash of color.

"I think we have to get back. We've been shaded by trees much of the time but the sun's strong."

"I agree. I need to shower and prepare for the next," he says.

"Next?" you say.

He finally smiles, looking less worried. "More surprises."

"Goody."

4:58 pm

You encourage Sándor to rest before you have to leave for dinner at six. It would have been easier if you hadn't brought so much stuff to wear. You like having choices but have to narrow it down. After a shower, you're still hot and it's muggy so you choose a sundress, black with cornflower blue paisleys on it, tea-length with thin strappy things at the shoulder. You could wear flip-flops but go with black espadrilles instead. After you're spiffied up you almost admire yourself in the mirror. Almost. You frown instead and tie your hair in a bun to get it off your sweaty neck.

Sándor stirs and goes in for his shower. After he's dressed you grab your clutch and open the door. "Are we ready?" you sing, using your opera voice.

"Yes. Let me escort you."

Sándor wears his usual khaki pants with a short-sleeved, aqua-colored polo shirt. He takes your arm and guides you to the car, then opens the door for you. You smile. You're going on a date with a handsome man who loves you.

You drive south along the canal to the next town, where you find a parking space and walk the few blocks to the restaurant. The building painted in different bright colors delights you. The sign says Authentic Mexican and Peruvian Cuisine.

The room is lit with dim lights and candles but the hostess takes you to the patio. By now it's cooler so you'll be comfortable outside. The waitress comes with a wine list and menu, and fills your empty glasses with water. Sándor hands her the list and keeps the menus, giving one to you.

There are pictures of many of the dishes on the menu and they all look delicious. Sándor knows what he wants already. You're still making up your mind when the waitress returns.

"You order first. By the time you're done I'll be ready," you say.

When you finish ordering Sándor sighs.

"Are you okay?" you say.

He reaches across the table and takes your hand. "I am not sure—something…" His eyes glaze over and his grip on your hand loosens.

"Sándor?"

After another moment, he shakes it off. "I am sorry."

"Did you have a vision?"

He looks at you but says nothing.

"Are you well enough to eat?"

"Yes. I am just dizzy."

The food arrives, large blue and yellow plates filled with meaty Peruvian fare. You eat with vigor. Sándor barely touches his, taking occasional sips of water. After you finish the main course he signals for the waitress and asks her to bring the dessert menu.

"Do you want to leave now and take dessert with us?" you say.

Sándor rubs his forehead and says, "That is a good idea."

8:19 pm

"I did not want our weekend to be a disappointment."

"It's been lovely." You kiss him. "How're you doing?"

"I am feeling better."

"I'll get dessert then." You move towards the table where the takeout containers are and Sándor follows, stopping you before you get there.

"My Dear—"

"Wha—"

He stops you with a kiss and carries you to the bed, where you snuggle and kiss one another. This time the urgency is gone, and you linger over one another.

Sunday, July 24th
9:47 am

You and Sándor take breakfast in the inn's dining room. The apple-cinnamon French toast melts in your mouth and goes beautifully with coffee.

"Yum. How'd you sleep?" you say.

"Well. I feel refreshed."

"Will you be okay for the drive?"

"Yes. Although the visions are never long, they exhaust me. Thank you for understanding."

"Can you tell me about it?"

"There is no point. I did not have a sense of time, and it could have come from my own anxiety."

You're almost finished eating when Nathan walks to your table and whispers into Sándor's ear. Then the sound of screaming interrupts you. You wonder what's going on. There's a brief silence, and then a louder din of bleating, shrill and labored, follows. You hold your hands over your ears and Sándor comes to your side of the table and puts his arm around your shoulders, knowing how sensitive to sound you are. You can't help it; your eyes well up.

"Alex, I am sorry. One of the sheep had to be put down." He helps you stand and takes you to the cottage. "Are you alright?"

"The sound startled me. I'm tired. Is it alright if we go now?"

"Of course."

You pack your things. It doesn't take long for Sándor to settle with Nathan and you make a fast departure. The ride home is long, and there's a lot of traffic on the highway. A hot Sunday in the summer, everyone is going to the beach for the day. You finally arrive at your condo. Sándor carries your luggage in. You hesitate to ask but you're scared so you ask anyway.

"Can you stay?"

"I am sorry, My Dear. I have a client."

"Ah, okay."

"I will see you soon. Get some rest."

"I'll pick Jeffrey up and get settled." You pause. "Thanks for the wonderful weekend," you say and kiss Sándor.

"You are welcome. I love you."

"Thank you. Me, too."

9:31 pm

You're just getting in bed when three sharp knocks startle you.

Sándor!

You close the bedroom door behind you so Jefferson won't come out. Sándor must have finished early and you open the front door without hesitating.

Zoltán shoves you inside, closes the door and locks the deadbolt. Then he takes a rope, ties your hands and moves you to the couch, where he stands in front of you. He's thinner, with hair straggling around his face. And he smells—ripe and gross like he hasn't bathed. You can't help wrinkling your nose in the midst of terror.

"What? You are not glad to see me?" he says.

All you can do is keep your head lowered and shake it.

Jefferson begins to howl.

"Who is going to save you this time? Surely not my foolish brother."

You look up again and glare.

"Where are the keys to your car?"

"They're in the bedroom. But Jefferson—"

"I do not care about the dog. I will take care of him if I have to."

You start to cry.

"Be quiet," he says, and moves down the hall.

Although your hands aren't free you get up and stagger to the front door. You can't reach the deadbolt. If you get to the slider you can go to the back yard, but don't want to leave Jeffrey, who yelps just as you slide the screen across. You run for the bedroom; Zoltán is just coming out.

"What did you do to my dog?" you snarl.

"I kicked him. He will stay quiet now."

Anger explodes in your head; your leg lashes out at Zoltán, who swings something at your head and you fall, blinded by blacks and reds.

You can't open your eyes. Your head hurts and you hear voices, although you can't move because you're choking, an arm latched onto your neck.

"Give me the gun. You have nowhere to go."

Sándor.

"Call them off or I will kill her," Zoltán says.

You open your eyes. Zoltán tightens his arm around your neck and drags you to the front door. You see the deck beyond the living room where policemen kneel, their guns pointed in your direction.

"It is over, my brother. Let her go," Sándor says.

Zoltán loosens his hold, takes you by the scruff of the neck and sticks the gun against your forehead.

You whimper.

Sándor takes a step back.

Zoltán cocks the trigger and says, "Neked csinálok, bátyám." He slams you against the wall, where you struggle to open your eyes.

He puts the gun in his mouth.

"No!" Sándor shouts.

Their eyes lock and Zoltán pulls the trigger.

Chapter Twenty-seven
Sunday, July 24th
7:01 am

You're afraid to open your eyes and although aware of where you are, your recollection is dim. Your head hurts. When you gather yourself and risk looking, the room is still dark; shades are drawn to keep out the glare of the morning sun. You're the only patient in the room and Sándor lies on the empty hospital bed next to yours, sleeping. You make it to the bathroom.

The bandage is loose and you peel it back, revealing an angry gash on your forehead—a trail of stitches holding the skin together. You wash your hands and splash water on your face. Your hair's a mess, still greasy from where they washed out Zoltán's blood. Last night they cleaned you up after they dressed the wound. You remember that much. Now you want to get away from here and go somewhere safe to have a hot shower.

When you return Sándor's sitting on the edge of the bed. He stands and meets you, then holds you close. The shock's wearing off, the horror of yesterday's gore coming back to you. Sándor's suffering. You know that, yet you still can't talk.

"I do not think you should go home," he says.

"I don't want to."

"Someone can come and clean tomorrow. For now, please tell me what you need and I will get it. Jefferson is already at my house."

All you can do is nod.

Tuesday, July 26th
6:32 pm

"Would you like another blanket?" Sándor says.

You shake your head and turn to face the window, pulling the covers over your head. Jefferson curls up behind you.

"Please text me if you need anything. I should not be too long." He kisses your hair and leaves.

A cleaning service came yesterday to scour your condo—Zoltán's blood splattered all over the walls by the front door. You spent today packing and let Sándor help; you were not able to stand being there without leaving the doors and windows open, and kept going outside for fresh air. Tomorrow the movers take the furniture to the storage unit—even the piano. You hate to part with it, but Sándor has a piano you like and yours will be safe in a climate-controlled environment.

Sándor returns from meeting his client and you finally speak. "I'm sorry I've been quiet. How are you doing with all of this? And how is László?"

After a few moments, he answers. "He was my brother, my twin. I ache from the loss of him—the connection is gone, his soul disintegrated. László is quiet, does not wish to talk."

"I'm sorry."

Sándor shrugs. "Zoltán moved onto the next, where he cannot cause harm any longer. It was his choice. He leaves behind a son and brother, who loved him in spite of his behavior. Now we must have time to heal."

He climbs in bed with you and Jefferson moves to your feet. You see your mother's portrait in the moonlight. She reassures you with her sweet smile and sympathetic eyes, beautiful and enduring. You sleep long into the night, beyond dawn until late morning.

Saturday, July 30th
9:53 am

You wake to shrieks of joy coming from down the hall—shower time for the parrot. The corners of your mouth lift; it's been a while since you smiled and you need it. László has been home since Sándor picked him up from football camp. He hasn't spoken of his father's death and stays in his room.

Sándor's been caring for you all week and now you must attend to him. By the time he finishes with György, you have breakfast ready. You're setting the table when he walks through the kitchen door.

"Should I make muffins, too, or are you okay with eggs and toast?"

"This is enough, My Dear."

You stay quiet as you have breakfast. Sándor helps you tidy up after and then goes to the slider by the deck, where you soon join him.

"What can I do for you?" you say.

"I will have to talk with him."

"I know. Would you like me to take off and give you some space?"

He slips his arm around your waist. "László will have to become accustomed to you. I want you here with us for as long as you wish to stay. He does not say much but likes you."

"And I like him. He's a good kid. I'm sorry about his father."

6:50 pm

By now the beach is less cluttered with people. You watch from the window as Sándor and László walk north on the sand and you send them thoughts of healing and compassion. Jefferson needs his final walk of the day; he's adjusted well to his new surroundings. You thought he'd be jealous of Sándor but he's been good, happy to have another human on hand to spoil him. Now he'll enjoy László as well. They're still not back when you get ready for bed. You've been going to bed early since it happened, now a week later.

Zoltán. You can't imagine having a father like him. But you know loss. He was a bad man, but still a father, a brother. You think of your own father. And Coach. Yes, you're acquainted with what happens when someone close is ripped out of your life.

Thursday, August 18th
3:16 am

The bed is hot from the heat of your body. Sándor sleeps next to you and stirs, sits up and kisses you. The taste of his mouth is foul and you open your eyes. *Zoltán.* You try to scream and he pulls your hair to shut you up. Terror sends chills up your spine and he reaches over you to the nightstand where there's a tall bottle of vodka. He pinches your nose and pours the vodka into your mouth as you struggle and kick at him. Zoltán is—or was—dead. This cannot be. He's torturing you and there's no way to—

"My Dear?" Sándor shakes you.

You're crying.

"You are safe, Alex. I am here. You were having another nightmare."

"Awful, just awful." You roll over to him. He cradles you in his arms and you arch your back, stretching away the stiffness of sleep.

He kisses your neck and your body relaxes.

"Alex," he whispers.

You kiss him, melt and your fear recedes.

"That is nice," he murmurs, and takes you in his arms.

It's been almost four weeks since your birthday, the weekend you went away with Sándor. Until now you've been sleeping in the same bed, but without any sexual intimacy. He's been patient and now it's time.

You lie awake for a long time after, relieved and less burdened, while Sándor snores. There's a familiarity about the gentle rhythm of snoring that reassures you.

Tuesday, September 6th
7:43 am

László's back in school. He made the varsity team this year and you and Sándor look forward to seeing some of his football games together. You have your own room in the house and meet Sándor in his room or he comes to yours at night. The household rides on a groove of routine; you wake next to Sándor, make breakfast for the three of you and then go your separate ways.

This morning before breakfast you busy yourself with photocopying scores of your requiem. Rehearsals begin tonight and All Soul's Day is less than two months away. You're excited and hum as you work. After you bind the scores you start breakfast.

Sándor hugs you from behind.

"I love you," he says.

You hesitate, then say, "Thanks."

László appears and sits at the table. "Good morning," he says.

"Hi," you say. "Would you like coffee this morning?"

"That might help."

Sándor puts a hand on László's shoulder. "Did you not rest well enough?"

"I guess not." László looks away, towards the ocean.

Sándor raises his eyebrows and frowns. "Would you like me to drive you to school today?"

"Nah, I'm okay. Gordy's mom's taking us."

You slide two eggs on László's plate, three on Sándor's and keep one for yourself. "Grapefruit anyone?"

László makes a face. "No, thanks."

"I would like a grapefruit," Sándor says.

You cut the fruit and split it with him. He devours it and rises to embrace László before he leaves for school. By the time you finish yours László is out the door.

6:59 pm

You're too nervous to sit in your seat, so you stand next to Maestro Healey as people file into the choir rehearsal room. "Are you ready for this?" he says.

"I think so—it's pretty exciting. Do you think we can do it?"

"With a lot of rehearsing, we can. We'll see how tonight goes. You may have to take the altos and sopranos to the church to rehearse them and I'll work with the men here. For now, I'll see how far we get with everyone together."

"Whatever's best," you say.

Healey starts near the beginning of the first movement, where the chorus enters after the solos. The ladies float above the chanting of the men, soft and ethereal, and as the men strengthen, the altos and sopranos fade out, swallowed by the increase in volume and rhythmic activity. They're reading the music well, and you hear their enthusiasm.

The second movement, the *Kyrie*, is more difficult, for the group as well as Healey.

"What did you do to me, Alex?" Healey says.

The chorus laughs, then you're all wowed as he negotiates the contrapuntal lines of the piano part with precision. He has to rehearse all parts individually, and although you make it through the movement, you'll have to return to it again and again to reinforce the difficult vocal passages.

Healey ends the rehearsal with your *Dies Irae*. The piano music of the introduction reminds you of the opening music from the movie *The Exorcist*. Your hair stands on end, and for a moment a splash of dark red shadows the music you're holding. You squint and rub your eyes, hoping nobody notices.

This movement doesn't go as well. It's short, but the choral part is challenging with the different voice parts crossing over and under one another with dissonant harmonies and syncopated rhythms. The chorus holds up well in spite of the difficulty of the music and as it begins to jell you have the chills again, wondering if anyone else has a similar reaction.

Rehearsal ends and you thank people as they leave. Then you approach Healey. "I think that went well. Anything you want me to change?"

"Not a thing. I think they'll enjoy it and will have no problem getting it ready for All Soul's Day."

As you drive home you can't get that *Dies Irae* out of your head. And you're grateful you won't have to sleep by yourself.

Friday, September 30th
11:47 pm

You wake, still moaning, the bedclothes soaked with your sweat. Sándor's hand presses on your forehead. "My Dear?" he says, nudging you.

"Horrible," you groan.

He turns on the light. "Do you remember it this time?"

"I remembered it last time, too. Trying not to."

It's always the same. In your dreams, you're drunk. When you awaken it's not only the fear of being drunk again—it's the way it happened. Zoltán forced it on you, a form of torture. Then you sit up, shaking. You have to tell Sándor. "He was there."

Sándor puts his arm around you. "I was wrong," he says.

"About what?"

"We should not speak of this in the night."

You shiver and wipe sweat off the back of your neck, terror gripping you. You have to know. "Aren't they just dreams?"

"I thought he would be gone, unable to break the barrier between this world and his. I was wrong. He is not at rest."

"What does that mean?" you say, and jump out of bed.

"They are more than dreams. Remembering allows him to become more present to you, take possession of you."

"What can I do?"

"I will cleanse the house. Then we should stay elsewhere for a short time."

"When do we have to go?"

"Soon. Next weekend, for a few days. That will give me time to prepare." He hugs you, encouraging you to get under the covers.

"Sándor?"

"Yes?"

"What did he say to you—just before—that thing in Hungarian?"

"He said, 'This I do for you, my brother.'"

"Do what?"

"I cannot be certain. Perhaps he took his life because he grew weary of it and wanted to try again in the next. Maybe he wanted to continue as spirit, move freely between worlds."

"Why?"

"Zoltán had many lovers but knew you and I would be together some day, bonded physically as well as on a soul level."

"So why would he kill himself and come back and haunt me?"

"He wants you because you are mine. I would not allow that to happen in this world and now he assaults you from the other."

You lay awake in his arms for a long time, shivering, until somewhere in the house a clock strikes three times.

Chapter Twenty-eight
Friday, October 7th
3:17 pm

"Who's been smoking dope?" you say.

Sándor smiles as he walks past you and moves beyond the kitchen carrying a smudge stick.

"It is sage, the same herb I used to make the cleanse of your condo."

"And that's gonna get rid of him?"

He opens the slider and kitchen window, allowing the breeze to blow the smoke around the house. "I will have to do more, especially the hallway and the bedrooms. I left glasses of salt water in every room. That will also absorb negativity."

"You didn't answer my question," you say.

Sándor lights a stick of incense. "Help me open all the doors and pray with intention."

"Intention?"

"Pray that the cleansing smoke will eliminate toxins."

You follow him down the hall, opening doors along the way. He moves from room to room waving the burning incense. "He will not like the aromas of sage and sandalwood. It may keep him from invading your dreams."

"Why do we have to leave?"

"Without your energy to feed off he will not come; that and the cleanse should protect the house from psychic attack."

"Oh." You're not convinced but play along. "So, when we get back Sunday afternoon I'll be safe?"

"That is my hope."

After László's football game you'll go to Cape May, where you have reservations at a B & B for the weekend. László will stay with his friend Gordy and family.

5:56 pm

On the way to the game, László says, "Look for me, number sixty-five."

"Have a good game," Sándor says.

"We're playing a good team. They'll be tough to beat."

"Have fun," you say.

You drop László off and he runs for the locker room when Sándor parks the car. It's early and you stroll around the neighborhoods nearby. You glance over your shoulder, the school in the distance behind you.

"Alex?"

"Uh-huh?"

"Is something wrong?"

"No, I'm just thinking about…" You stay quiet.

"It is alright for you to remember," Sándor says.

You take his hand and walk slower. "One time, after Max and I were together about a year, I spent the day with him at school and read *The Raven* to his English classes for Halloween."

He smiles. "That must have been dramatic."

"It was fun. I hammed it up, wore a crushed velvet black dress so I looked the part."

"Alexandra McRaven."

"Ha. I didn't think about that at the time. My name sounds like a character from one of Poe's stories. His work is dear to me—so graphic and vivid—*The Raven*, especially."

"How did the classes like it?"

"It got them off the hook—no schoolwork that day. What I noticed most was how they focused on Max during the question and answer session after I read. Kids pretend to be cool and often don't react much. He drew them out and his energy was contagious."

"In what way, contagious?"

"They were eager to discuss the poem—things like the supernatural atmosphere of it and themes of lost love. Then there's the raven with his unvarying response, 'Nevermore.' Coach knew the poem well and was able to quote from it. I could tell how much the kids respected him."

"I am not surprised," Sándor says.

You shake your head and wipe your eyes. "Let's head to the field. We want good seats in the bleachers."

In the first quarter, László stands on the sideline, cheering as the offense moves down the field after the opening kickoff. The Mustangs score on a short pass, and the coach puts László in the game at the kickoff for the second quarter. The other team has the ball and László gets the first hit; two of his teammates join in on the tackle on the twenty-seven-yard line. You and Sándor spring out of your seats and cheer for László, who trades high fives with the rest of the team on his way to the sideline. The clock runs down to zero and the teams make their way to the locker rooms at halftime. Sándor leaves to use the restroom.

Alone on the bench, you can't help thinking. These are kids who learned to play football under Coach; they didn't make it to the varsity team without playing for his freshman team first. The two seasons you were with Coach you went to see the freshman games, mostly because you enjoyed gawking at him—the look of his legs under the sleek coaching uniform, his groovy shades gleaming in the sunlight and—the intensity and energy he brought on the field as he interacted with the kids.

You smile, and before you can control it, tears pool in your eyes—his passion for you, his constant support and strength, enthusiasm for things you enjoyed doing together, the intimacy you shared—if you had a chance do it over you'd marry him, even knowing he was going to die.

He's gone almost a year. Today you watch the game with Sándor, who sideswiped your car just in time to carry you through the losses of Coach and your father, the mayhem that followed, your drinking and neglect of the world around you.

Sándor approaches, carrying four hotdogs in one hand, a coffee in the other.

You laugh. “Are those all for me?”

“I will share with you.” He sits and hands you the coffee and one hotdog.

László is on the field for the kickoff starting the second half. The Mustangs score again in the fourth quarter and win. After the game, you wait for László in the parking lot and soon he trots to the car.

“What a game,” you say.

Sándor hugs László. “Congratulations.”

“Did you see me tackle that guy?”

“Yes, we sure did!” you say.

“Our coaches were happy with us.”

Sándor smiles, proud of his nephew. Their love for one another gives you hope, and you want to cry again—relieved to be a part of that.

The three of you pile in the car, quiet until you reach Gordy’s house. As you pull up to the curb, Sándor says, “What is that smell?”

Your face reddens; you hope it wasn’t you.

“There he goes again,” László says.

“Blame the hotdogs,” Sándor says.

Sunday, October 9th
11:16 am

“Why are we taking the long way?” you say.

“I want to give the house more time for negativity to depart but arrive home in time for László,” Sándor says.

You shift your seat back and lean into it. “At least most of the tourists are gone. Ocean Drive is nuts in the summer.”

"Yes."

You're cranky and worry the nightmares won't go away. With Sándor many things are possible but Zoltán is his match, even from the realm of the dead. After a great weekend, you're sad it's over. Balmy weather let you amble on the beach and around town, browsing through shops, eating too much—and sleeping uninterrupted.

Shortly after you get home László comes in and goes to his room. You'll help him with his English paper later while Sándor has clients.

Wednesday, October 19th
8:02 am

"How was the rehearsal last night?" Sándor says.

"Went well. We're cutting one of the sections so we can give more attention to the primary parts of the mass. A few movements are solo, duet or ensembles, so we won't have to take rehearsal time for them. It's coming along."

"That is good. We should celebrate."

"Yes, for productive rehearsals and better sleep," you say.

"You have not had the nightmares."

"Not since you cleansed the house."

You hug him and he kisses you.

"I do not have a client for a few hours," he says.

"Your room or mine?"

He takes your hand and guides you to his room.

You and Sándor take your time, switching positions, laughing when you bump heads or become tangled in the bedclothes. Jefferson lies on the floor under the skylight; you pause and wave at him. He yawns and turns the other way.

Sunday, October 23rd
11:43 am

Healey always finds something appropriate, yet juicy enough for you, to coincide with the scripture readings. Today the choir sings, "How Lovely is Thy Dwelling Place," from Brahms' *Ein Deutches Requiem*. You sing it in English and it still packs a punch. It runs through your head as you drive home until you get sick of it and turn on the radio. *Dancing Queen* by Abba assaults your ears. You recover and sing along. Then it occurs to you.

You find Sándor in the kitchen making cheeseburgers for lunch. "Hey," you say.

"Hi."

"I've got an idea."

"Oh?"

"How about a party?"

He flips a burger and says, "For Halloween?"

"Yeah. Get this. We should have a dance-themed costume party."

"Brilliant. I will put the word out. How is this Saturday?"

"Sounds like a plan."

Saturday, October 29th
7:03 pm

László and Sándor roll the piano to the corner of the room and put away the area rugs, exposing the stone floor—great for dancing. You decorate and the house is alive with orange and purple strings of lights, glowing jack-o-lanterns and various creatures dangling from the ceiling—bats, cats, spiders and of course, ravens. A disco ball glitters from where it hangs. Cider and spiced wine mull on the stove, making the house smell of autumn.

"Quite festive, My Dear. They will love it," Sándor says, opening the slider. "We will keep the door open so everyone may move to the deck easily if they want; it will be hot in here with so many."

"Who's coming?"

"A few of my clients, who may also bring friends."

"More the merrier."

"And," he says.

"What?"

"László is going to a party with a friend."

"Who, Gordy?"

"He did not tell me but I suspect she will soon come for him."

"László has a girlfriend!"

He nods and smiles just as the doorbell rings.

"Aha," he says.

Before Sándor can react, László bounds into the room and stops short. He wears jeans and black ankle boots, a bright orange shirt under a long leather vest with fringes, and John Lennon glasses. "I'll get it," he says.

"Certainly," Sándor says and smiles, watching László step toward the kitchen entrance of the house. You and Sándor wait as László answers the bell.

She's almost as tall as you, wearing a pink, knee-length dress with long, flowing sleeves, white knee-high boots and beads. Long blond hair sets off the outfit. She walks through the door and says, "I'm Sylvia. Hi, László."

"Hey," he says, and smiles under a blush, rooted to his position.

"We're going to dance all night," she says.

"Dance?" László says, and swallows, running a hand through his curly hair.

She laughs.

You walk forward and stretch out your hand. "I'm Alex. Great costume."

Sándor smiles and kisses her on each cheek. "I am glad to meet you. Happy Halloween."

László recovers. Sylvia takes his hand and leads him out the door.

"She will be good for him," Sándor says.

"I like her, too," you say.

"I will go to the deck and get the fire started." He gives you a squeeze and then leaves.

You go to your room to dress. First, you let your hair out of the ponytail, goop it with mousse and scrunch it up. You're satisfied as it waves around your face and below your shoulders. Then you apply dark red lipstick, eyeliner and mascara, along with a choker at your neck with silver spikey things sticking out. You put on a black tank top and leather pants, boots and a leather jacket cropped at the waist with lots of zippers. You're ready to rumble.

When you see Sándor your eyes widen. He wears a pale blue suit with the jacket open, a white shirt with pointy collars underneath; the pants look like they've been painted on his body, and they flare at the bottom. You'll have trouble keeping your hands off him.

"Guess I have to wait until later," you say into his ear.

He kisses you. "It is a date."

Your iPod is loaded with a long playlist of songs from the 1960s, 70s and 80s, from classic rock to disco, metal to punk and new wave. You start the music. *It's the End of the World as We Know It* by R.E.M. plays—*Lenny Bruce is not afraid*— as the doorbell rings again; Sándor boogies through the kitchen and lets the first of the partygoers in.

He introduces you to three of his friends, and one of them, who wears a pile of gold chains around his neck, says, "Whoa. You are so Joan Jett. I pity the fool."

"Thanks, Mr. T. You look great," you say, and shake hands with him and his friends, one of whom looks like Frank Zappa with his signature facial hair. The woman with them wears a sleek purple suit with a ruffled shirt, reminiscent of Prince. Sándor embraces the two men and kisses the woman's hand.

He leads them to the kitchen with offers of cider or wine, and then they step out on the deck. As you wait for Sándor, the smell of spiced wine turns your stomach; you go to the slider for fresh air.

There are about twenty-five people at the party; the house doesn't feel crowded. You circulate, talking and dancing, first with two guys dressed like the rock group Kiss who have painted faces and leather like yours, and then a man in drag resembling Tina Turner—heals and everything—joins you.

*We can dance if we want to, we can leave your friends behind, cuz your friends don't dance and if they don't dance, well…*You bounce in time to the music, happy where you are, the smell of wine gone.

Jefferson prances into the room and mingles, checking everyone out, pausing when someone pets him. He sniffs at the table where the food is, snags a half-full bag of potato chips, carries it through the kitchen and down the hall. You let him have his fun.

10:57 pm

The party's hopping; you and Sándor have a chance to get together. *Oh, as long as I know how to love, I know I'll stay alive, I've got all my life to live, I've got all my…I will survive.* He towers over you and the others on the floor, becoming a focal point of the action. A circle forms around the two of you.

As Sándor moves in time to the music with his limbs flailing about, the lights flicker and the next song starts. He pauses, looks around for a moment, and then continues, this time encouraging everyone to form a conga line behind him.

The line snakes through the house, out to the deck and back again, gaining momentum from the beat of the music. *C'mon, c'mon, c'mon, c'mon now touch me, babe. Can't you see that I am not afraid. What was that promise that you made.* The shuffle-

shuffle-shuffle kick of the line becomes a presence, unifying the dancers as they begin to sing. *I'm gonna love you, till the heavens stop the rain*. The movement intensifies, stomp-stomp-stomp kick.

You're woozy and can't get your bearings. *I'm gonna love you, till the stars fall from the sky, for you and*—the power goes out.

Half the line is in the house and the other on the deck. Before anyone panics, Sándor moves next to the fire pit where you all can see him in the glow of the flames. In the quiet you hear people talking but don't know what they're saying because—

SLAM!

—the sudden, sick feeling of an urge to drink floods your senses.

"Make a circle around the fire," Sándor says.

The crowd doesn't question him. You can't move until your stomach twists into a knot that pulls you away from people, and the light. Sándor doesn't notice you're in the kitchen—where the alcohol is.

If you even taste it, you won't be able to stop.

Alex.

It's just a whisper in your head, but you know who it is.

Zoltán's presence courses through you, and you're paralyzed, queasy and disoriented, legs quivering. Sweat drips into your eyes.

Have a drink, Alex.

The kitchen cabinet rattles, where what little alcohol there is in the house is hidden. You haven't thought of it until now and don't want to move because you'll open the door and that'll be it.

Alex.

Spiced wine be damned. The hard stuff waits, a bottle of vodka, used for cooking. You stare at the door and it creaks open; you hesitate, shaking.

Go, ahead, Alex.

You stoop and reach for the bottle; it's almost full, heavy with poison. As you tilt it back and lift it to your lips you start sobbing.

"Alex!" The force of Sándor's voice diffuses the turmoil in your stomach.

You drop the bottle before you drink any of it, then stoop to clean it up.

"Leave it." Sándor says.

You rub tears out of your eyes.

"Come." Sándor carries two bundles of sage in one hand, takes yours with the other and leads you to the deck. The fire burns brighter, rising high.

The partygoers dance in a circle, rotating clockwise. The flames crackle and surge—*Oh, someone's waiting, just for you, spinning wheel, spinning through, drop all your troubles by the riverside, ride a painted pony let the spinning wheel fly-y-y*. The power is on; music jars you alert.

Sándor tosses a bundle into the fire. An explosion snaps everyone to a halt. A flaming shape emerges, struggling to take form. You don't know if anyone else can see it, but you can, and the specter of Zoltán lashes towards you. You stumble backwards out of his grasp, dizzy and faint, and squint your eyes shut. When you flip them open again the Zoltán-thing surrounds you, and you feel the icy heat of his sparking silhouette.

Sándor pulls you up, sets you on your feet and lobs the other bundle into the smoking fire. The blaze swirls upward, the Zoltán-thing with it, towering towards the sky above. As it ascends the shape of Zoltán intensifies and then stretches like the tail of a meteor, climbing higher. You think you hear him scream, then he flickers and disappears.

Chapter Twenty-nine
Sunday, October 30th
12:13 am

The clapping continues, and Sándor bows. Embers remain and the fire is gone. Applause tapers off and people start to leave, talking about the spectacular display. You're numb, but manage to say goodbyes as they go out the door.

The house is finally empty and László arrives. "Sorry I'm late," he says.

"That is okay. Did you enjoy the party?" Sándor says.

"Yeah. I had to dance."

"How could that be so horrible with such a beautiful partner?"

László reddens. "It wasn't so bad," he says and heads for his room.

Sándor turns to you. "My Dear—"

"I'm so sorry." You cover your eyes and shake your head. "What happened out there?"

"I knew it was too easy, his departure from your dreams. When he came this night, I was prepared."

"You made it look planned." You pause. "But did it work?"

"Zoltán attempted to use the energy of the fire to materialize. With the burning of the sage it had the opposite effect, purifying his soul rather than feeding his negativity."

"I can't wrap my mind around that," you say, and sob, with dumb thoughts of the immolation scene from the end of the opera, *Götterdämmerung*.

Sándor embraces you.

Wednesday, November 2nd
7:28 pm

Rex.

The piano punctuates the repetitions of the Latin word for *King* with chords in the lowest bass and highest treble registers of the instrument.

Rex.

Rex tremendae majestatis.

The chorus appeals to the King of tremendous majesty. Toward the end, a quartet of soprano, alto, tenor and bass soloists intone the words, *save me, source of mercy*, and their voices soar, soft and gentle, over a simple variation on the chords from the beginning, gradually becoming less present.

The next two movements are for ensemble voices and the rest of the chorus sits. This gives you the opportunity to fret about your solo, near the end of the requiem. This time you won't have to accompany yourself because Maestro Healey will do it. You'll have to face the audience and won't be able to preoccupy yourself with playing.

A trio sings: *I moan as one who is guilty...Provide me a place among the sheep, and separate me from the goats, guiding me to Your right hand.* You think about the words too much. They sing in Latin but you know what it means. *Separate me from the goats*—creepy. Are you a lamb, or a goat?

The *Confutatis*, feisty and dramatic, gives you a kick; the beginning reminds you of Mozart and the end, with its chanting of the chorus in unison, is reminiscent of Carl Orff, another favorite composer of yours.

A few sections later, the chorus sings the *Sanctus, Holy, Holy, Holy, Lord God of Hosts*. The lilting, tonal phrases of the music give the audience the first tune the ear grasps easily, with material that returns throughout the movement. A few people even applaud at the end. They're lulled into a false sense of comfort; your *Agnus Dei* solo is next.

With Healey accompanying you, it's easier to sing than it was for your father's memorial service and your voice is cleaner than it's been in years. You notice Sándor sitting in the front row and you smile as you sing, although the words are somber. His eyes grow bigger at your low notes in the closing phrases, *grant them eternal rest forever.* You sing well and Healey nails the accompaniment; the audience does not applaud after. And that's okay with you.

The chorus recesses to the choir loft to sing the final movement with the organ instead of in front of the congregation with the piano. Healey pulls out all the stops, which delights you, and the rich singing of the chorus fills the church.

Lux. Lux aeterna. Let eternal light shine upon them, Lord.

The congregation stands and applause rings in your head. Father Marcus points toward the loft, waving you downstairs. You ask everyone to come with you and go with Healey, the chorus following. Father presents you with a bouquet as the clapping continues. You acknowledge Maestro Healey and the chorus; soloists step forward to take bows. With a burst of fervor, you hug Father and Healey, thanking them both. Tears fill your eyes as you take your own bow.

Monday, November 14th
7:02 pm

László and Sylvia walk ahead while you and Sándor dally. There isn't much beach but enough that you can stay on the sand without getting wet. The moon is full in the clear sky, rising over the ocean.

Jefferson struts down the beach, now accustomed to the evening walks. György flies from Sándor's shoulder and lands briefly on the beagle's back, then hops along beside him in the sand—parrot and dog, unlikely friends.

You have to laugh, and then smile at Sándor.

“I am proud of you,” he says.

“Thank you. I feel the same about you.” You pinch his butt before you take his hand. “And not just because you’re so handsome.”

He laughs. “Your requiem was a success. Will you continue with the opera for children?”

“I’m a little burned out, but yes. I have almost a year.”

“There is time, then.”

Your belly’s full and you love these walks. Sylvia came by after László’s football practice to have dinner because they’re working together on a project for school and want to brainstorm with you.

You love Sándor. He makes that easy. You want to tell him but as always, it’s difficult to say.

“Sanyi?”

“Yes?” He smiles down at you.

“I do love you, you know.” It wasn’t easy, but you said it—before he did.

He picks you up and spins you around.

Tuesday, November 22nd
9:17 pm

You light a candle, lower your head and say a prayer; then you stare at the flame for a while, watching it dance in the breeze from the ceiling fan. It’s Coach’s birthday. Thoughts of him don’t preoccupy you often, or fill you with regret, although you haven’t forgotten. The only way you can think of to offer him amends is by giving to others, and accepting what’s given you—affection, love, compassion, and a healthy lifestyle—all things you denied yourself, and Coach, while he lived. You don’t want to screw things up with Sándor—

Knock, knock.

“Come on in.” You run to the door and hug Sándor.

"All is well?" He sits on the edge of the bed with you.

Except for the candle, it's dark. Sándor doesn't know everything but knows when not to talk. You put your head on his shoulder and Jefferson hops up, squeezing between you.

The portrait of your mother hangs on the wall. It's the first thing you notice when you get up in the morning; now it's difficult to see, as if memories of her are fading. You know that's not the case; it's the pain associated with that time in your life that's growing dimmer. Now, you remember times when you, your mother and father went to the opera, times when you sat with them by the fire at home or traveled together.

With the exception of nightmares and Halloween party with Zoltán's devilry, you haven't thought much about hoo-hah. And you don't miss it. Moments go by and you stay in them, no longer anticipating dread around every corner.

You recall the book Sándor gave you, *Talking with Angels*. Its greatest idea is that joy is within you. It's always been there, although until now you couldn't embrace it. You can't get over how simple it is. You *are* the joy.

Jefferson rests his paw on your arm, stretches and yawns. You snuggle closer to Sándor, who doesn't stir. You enjoy the warm glow from the candle until it burns out, and sleep.

The End

Made in the
USA
Middletown, DE

73948740R00149